THE GRAYWOLF SHORT FICTION SERIES

1 9 9 2

ALSO BY PATRICIA HENLEY

Learning to Die (Poetry, 1979)
Friday Night at Silver Star (Stories, 1986)

THE Secret OF Cartwheels

SHORT STORIES BY

Patricia Henley

GRAYWOLF PRESS

The stories in this book were originally published in the following periodicals, to whose editors grateful acknowledgment is made: Fiction '87, the Boston Globe Sunday Magazine, the Atlantic, Cutbank, Sycamore Review, Ploughshares, Colorado Review, and Mississippi Valley Review. "Sid Ol' Kid," words and music by Bob Merrill, copyright © 1957 Golden Bell Songs, used by permission of Hal Leonard Publishing Corporation. The author wishes to thank K.R. and the Department of English at Purdue University for their support during the completion of this manuscript.

Publication of this volume is made possible in part by a grant provided by the Minnesota State Arts Board, through an appropriation by the Minnesota State Legislature, and by a grant from the National Endowment for the Arts. Additional support has been provided by the Jerome Foundation, the Northwest Area Foundation, the Mellon Foundation, the Lila Wallace/ Reader's Digest Fund, and other generous contributions from foundations, corporations, and individuals. Graywolf Press is a member agency of United Arts, Saint Paul. To these organizations and individuals who make our work possible, we offer heartfelt thanks.

Published by G R A Y W O L F   P R E S S
2402 University Avenue, Suite 203
Saint Paul, Minnesota 55114
Printed in the United States of America

9 8 7 6 5 4 3 2

Library of Congress Cataloging-in-Publication Data
Henley, Patricia.
        The secret of cartwheels : short stories / by Patricia Henley.
            p.   cm.
        ISBN 1-55597-168-7 (pbk.) : $11.00
        1. West (U.S.) – Fiction.   I. Title.
    PS3558.E49633S4   1992
    813'.54 – dc20   92-14989

for my brothers and sisters,
Michael, Nancy, Mary Ruth,
Stephen, David, Margaret Ann,
and George

Contents

You who knelt on the frozen leaves,
You who know how dark it got under the ice;
You know how hard it was to live
with hatred, how long it took to convert
death and sadness into beautiful singing.

— Gerald Stern, "Singing"

The Secret of Cartwheels

THE WINESAP TREES along the road were skeletal in the early evening light. I stared out the school bus window and cupped like a baby chick the news I looked forward to telling Mother: I'd decided on my confirmation name.

"What's nine times seven?" Jan Mary said.

"Sixty-three," I said. *Joan.* That was Mother's confirmation name, and I wanted it to be mine as well. She'd told me it was a name of strength, a name to carry you into battle.

"I tore my cords," Christopher said. He stood in the aisle, bracing himself with one hand on the chrome pole beside the driver, who wore a baseball cap and a big plaid mackinaw.

The bus driver sang, "Don't sit under the apple tree with anyone else but me." I knew we were nearing our stop, the end of the route, whenever the driver sang this song. We were the last ones on the bus. Although the heater was chuffing hard, frost in the shape of flames curled along the edges of the windows.

"Sweet dreams," the driver said, as we plodded down the slippery steps of the school bus.

Aunt Opal's pale green Cadillac was parked at an odd angle near the woodshed. I knew something was wrong – she never drove out from Wenatchee to visit in the winter. I remembered what our mother had told me the night before. Before bedtime we all lined up to kiss her good night, and when my turn came, she'd said, "There are signs in life. Signs that tell you what you have to do." Her voice had frightened me. I didn't want to hear what she had to say.

Jan Mary said, "Who's that?" Her knit gloves were soggy, her knees chapped above slipping down socks.

"Aunt Opal," Christopher said. His voice was dead and I knew he knew and understood.

Our breath came in blue blossoms in the cold, cutting air, and a light went on in the living room. I didn't want to go in, but I kept trudging through the snow.

Inside, everything was in its place, but our mother was gone, which made the house seem cold and empty. Four-year-old Suzanne stood on the heat register, her grubby chenille blanket a cape around her shoulders. Her hair had been recently brushed, and she wore plastic barrettes, a duck on one side, a bow on the other. When I remember those years at home, this is one of the things I focus on, how nothing ever matched, not sheets, not barrettes, not cups and saucers, not socks. And sometimes I think the sad and petty effort to have matching things has been one of the chief concerns of my adult life. Aunt Opal perched uneasily on a ladder-back chair with the baby, Laura Jean, on her lap. Laura Jean, eyes roving, held her own bottle of milk, and when she saw me, her look latched on to me and she stopped sucking and squirmed and kicked. Her plastic bottle clunked onto the floor. Aunt Opal's white wool pantsuit stretched tightly across her fat thighs. Her teased hair stood hard and swirled. Ill-at-ease, she shifted her weight gingerly as though she might get dirty. I thought I saw pity in her eyes, and I looked away. Christopher and Jan Mary hung back by the kitchen door, Christopher banging his metal lunch box softly against his leg.

"Where's our mother?" I said, scooping Laura Jean away from Aunt Opal.

"Now I hate to have to be the bearer of bad tidings," she began. "I know this will be hard on you children. I don't know what your mother was thinking of." She got up and stalked over to Suzanne, her spike heels dragging on the linoleum.

"Just tell me where she is." The baby stiffened in my arms. This was the first time I'd ever issued a command to a grown-up, and I felt both powerful and worried. Without our mother there, I was suddenly older.

Aunt Opal took a few seconds to adjust one of Suzanne's barrettes. "At the VA hospital," she said. "She's sick. Surely you must have known? She needs a rest. She's gone away and left you."

Christopher and Jan Mary went meek as old dogs into the living room and turned on the television. I snugged the baby into her high chair, wrapped a receiving blanket around her bare legs, and began peeling potatoes for supper. Suzanne sat in her miniature rocker, holding a Dr. Seuss book upside down and mouthing the words she knew by heart. I remember thinking if we could just have an ordinary supper, do our homework, fold the laundry, say our prayers, then it would be all right with mother away. We might feel as though she'd just gone through the orchard to visit a neighbor, and that she might return at any moment.

"You'll have places to go, of course," Aunt Opal said, lighting the gas under the stale morning coffee. The sulphurous smell of the match lingered.

"Places?"

"Christopher can stay with Grandma and Grandpa. Janice will take the baby."

"We'll stay here together," I said.

"Roxanne," she said, pouring coffee into a flowered teacup.

"You can't stay here alone with all these children."

I remember feeling small and powerless then, and I saw that I still needed to be taken care of–in fact, wanted to be taken care of–but I did not think I would be. I had no trust in anyone, and when you are a child feeling this way, every day becomes a swim through white water with no life jacket. Many years went by before I allowed myself to wonder where my father was during this time.

"How long will we be gone?" I said.

"It's hard to say," Aunt Opal said, sighing. "It's really hard to say."

I was thirteen, Christopher twelve, and Jan Mary eight. We went to St. Martin's and rode the public school bus home, aware of our oddity–Christopher's salt-and-pepper cords instead of jeans, the scratchy scapulars against our chests, the memorization of saints' names and days and deeds. The week before our mother went away, I had stayed home from school twice, missing play auditions and report card day. She had written excuses on foolscap: *Please excuse Roxanne from school yesterday. I needed her at home.*

Our father worked in another state. The house was isolated, out in the country; our nearest neighbor lived a mile away. During the summer I loved where we lived–the ocean of apple blooms, the muted voices of the Spanish-speaking orchard workers, the wild berries, like deep black fleece along the railroad tracks. Winters were another story. We heated with wood, and the fine wood ash smudged our schoolbooks, our clothes and linens, our wrists and necks. The well was running dry, and we children shared our bathwater. By my turn the water was tepid and gray. Our mother fed the fire, waking sometimes twice in the night to keep it going, and her hands and fingers were cracked, swollen. I wanted to cry whenever I looked at them. The loneliness was like a bad smell in the house.

In the evening while the others, the younger ones, watched "I Love Lucy," she sipped Jack Daniel's from a jelly glass and told me her secrets, plucking me from childhood's shore. Very late, when the others had gone to bed, she'd curse our father in a whisper. One night, when she had filled that jelly glass for the third time, and wanted company, she told me about her true love, a woman she'd known in the WACS during the war when they worked together in the motor pool in Dayton, Ohio. You can learn too much too soon about your mother's past. The weight of her concerns made me turn from her and wish that something would save us from the life we shared with her. I couldn't make the wish while watching her split and bleeding hands light a cigarette. But later, lying confused and rigid in the double bed I shared with cuddling Jan Mary and Suzanne, I wished that our mother would go away.

ALL OF THE MOVING took place at night. Aunt Opal drove Suzanne, Jan Mary, and me up the Entiat River to Entiat Home, a place local people called the orphans' home, but in truth the children there were not orphans but children whose parents could not care for them. The frozen river glittered in the moonlight. The fir trees rode in dark procession along the far bank. I sat in the front seat, a privilege of the oldest. The car was vast and luxurious and foreign. Most of the way, no one spoke.

Finally, from the cavernous backseat, Suzanne said, "Where's the baby?"

Don't ask, I thought, don't ask. I tried to send this silent message to Suzanne, but she didn't get it. Blood beat in my head.

"Laura Jean might need us," she said.

"Laura will be fine. Fine, fine," Aunt Opal said. "She's with your cousin Janice, who has another baby for her to play with."

Her jolly voice made me feel as though someone was hugging me too hard, painfully. When we'd left Christopher at Grandma and Grandpa Swanson's I'd felt sick to my stomach, not because I would be separated from him – no – but because I wanted to stay there too. I wanted to cling to Grandma Swanson and say, Take me, keep me. But I was the oldest. I didn't cling and cry.

I would miss Christopher. We had fallen into the habit of sitting in the unfinished knotty-pine pantry, after our baths and the dishes were done, listening to the high-school basketball games on the staticky radio. We knew the players' names and numbers. Together we had anticipated the mystery of going to high school.

Aunt Opal turned slowly into the uphill drive, which was lined with billows of snow. The dark was my comfort – I didn't want to see everything at once. We parked in front of a red brick house with two wrought iron lamps beside the neatly shoveled steps. Silence leaped at us when Aunt Opal shut off the engine. The place seemed a last outpost before the black and convoluted mountains, the Cascades, which, I imagined, went slanted and ragged to the sea. Then quickly, nimbly, a man and woman came coatless down the steps and opened the car doors, greeting us as though we were their own children returning home. The woman was thin and wore pearls and a skirt and sweater. The man had hair as black as an eggplant. Their voices were cheerful, but they kept their hands to themselves, as though they knew we would not want to be touched by strangers.

One moment we were in the dark, the car, the winter mountain air; the next, all three of us were ushered into the blinding white room, which was like a hospital room, with white metal cupboards, white metal cots, and everything amazingly clean and shiny under the fluorescent lights, cleaner even than Grandma Swanson's house.

We sat on the edge of one cot without speaking to one another. Snow dripped in dirty puddles from our saddle oxfords. The floor was black and white like a checkerboard. In the hallway, out of sight, Aunt Opal spoke with the man and woman – "Well behaved," I heard her say – and then she departed with all the speed and indifference of a UPS driver. Through a tall window in the room I watched her headlights sweep across the cinnamon bark of a ponderosa pine. From someplace faraway in the house came Christmas carols, wreathed in pure recorded voices. My body played tricks on me; my head hurt; my stomach knotted in an acid snarl.

Suzanne growled in a baby way she had when she was tired or angry. I pulled her onto my lap and she sucked her thumb. Consoling her was my only source of reassurance.

Jan Mary stamped the dirty puddles with the toe of her shoe. "How will we get to school?" she said.

"We'll go to a different school."

"I don't want to."

"We don't always get to do what we want," I said, shocked at the way I parroted our mother.

The woman in the pearls came into the bright room and leaned over us, one arm around Jan Mary's back.

"I'm Mrs. Thompson," she said. Her words were stout with kindness, which seemed a warning to me, as though she could hurt me, and she smelled good, like flowery cologne. She's someone's perfect mother, I thought.

"You'll need baths before bedtime, girls," she said. She strode to the oak door across the room and opened it, then switched on the bathroom light. "You have your own pajamas?"

"Yes," I said, nodding in the direction of the cardboard

Cream of Wheat carton, which held my clothes. Each of us had packed a carton with our best things.

"You can help your sisters bathe, Roxanne," she said. "Then I'll check your heads for lice."

"Our mother wouldn't allow that," I said.

"What did you say?"

"Our mother wouldn't allow us to have lice," I said. My voice seemed inordinately loud.

"It's just our policy," she said. "Now get moving. It's late."

We bedded down the first night in that same room, on the single cots made up with coarse cotton sheets and cream-colored wool blankets with a navy stripe around the edge. The light from the hallway bridged the high transom of the closed door, and I didn't sleep for a long time. Our presence there rebuked our mother, and I felt that humiliation as keenly as though I were she. I kept thinking, We'll be better when we go home – we'll work harder, knock down the cobwebs more often, check Jan Mary's homework, throw out the mismatched socks. Keeping domestic order was, inexplicably, bound up with being good, blessed. The fantasies that lulled me to sleep were of cupboards packed with thick folded towels, full cookie jars, an orderly abundance like perpetual fire against the night.

The next morning I lay there, warm but wet, with the covers up to my neck. Suzanne and Jan Mary were still asleep. A cat meowed urgently in the hallway. The windows were long and divided into panes of wavery old glass. Outside it was snowing; the dry, fine net of winter. There was an old cottonwood tree in the yard that had been struck by lightning some time ago. The split in the main trunk had been girdled with an iron band; it had healed, and now the scar tissue bloomed over the edge of the metal ring. I wondered what time it was and what would happen next. The procedure of moving, being dropped off like a litter of kittens, had been bad enough, and now I had to admit I'd wet the bed. I dreaded telling someone, but wanted to get it over with.

I thought of Mary in *The Secret Garden* and the way her spite protected her. I remembered the places I'd read the book: on the school steps at recess in second grade, under the cooling arms of a juniper tree when I was eleven. My own spite and anger could not protect me. They were repulsive thoughts I couldn't bear to admit to myself, because then I'd have to admit them to the priest. I'd told him once that I'd wished our mother would go away. I'd wished it for my birthday, which seemed to magnify the sin. He did not understand the power of wishes, and for penance he gave me a mere five Hail Marys. And now our mother *was* gone and I tried to imagine her inside the VA Hospital, but I could only picture the rusted iron bars, the flaking pink stucco walls. It was down by the Columbia River. The summer I was ten, a male patient people called *a crazy* had deliberately walked into the river and drowned.

The door opened, Mrs. Thompson peeked in, and Jan Mary and Suzanne sat up in their cots, their choppy hair all askew, eyes puffy with sleep.

"Time to get up, ladies," Mrs. Thompson said. She wore a robe of some soft peach fabric.

"Snow," Suzanne announced.

I threw back the covers, and the cool air sliced through my wet pajamas and chilled me. I forced myself to slither across the floor.

"Mrs. Thompson," I said officiously, as though I spoke of someone else, "I've wet the bed."

"Oh?"

"What shall I do?"

She stepped into the room and closed the door. "Does this

happen often?" She walked to my cot, with me close behind.

"Roxie wet the bed, Roxie wet the bed," Jan Mary sang.

I flung her a murderous glare, which silenced her at once.

"Sometimes," I said vaguely. By this time I had no feelings in the matter. I'd killed them, the way you track down a mud dauber and squash him.

Mrs. Thompson quickly jerked the sheets from the bed and carried them into the bathroom, holding them at arm's length from her peachy robe.

"Please," I said. "Let me."

She dumped the sheets in the tub. "Run cold water on them. Add your pajamas. Rinse them good. Ask your sister to help you wring them out and then hang them over this shower curtain. When they dry, we'll put them in the dirty laundry." I felt I'd depleted whatever good will there'd been between us.

The entire six months at Entiat I followed this routine. I managed to keep from wetting the bed four times in that six months, by what miracle I could not tell. I tried prayers and wishes, not drinking after six in the evening. Nothing worked. I lived in the Little Girls' House, though my age was border-line – they could have assigned me to the Big Girls' House. And every day all the little girls knew what I'd done when they saw my slick and gelid sheets hanging like Halloween ghosts in the bathroom.

Mrs. Hayes, the dorm mother of the Little Girls' House, had two immense tomcats, Springer and Beau, whose claws had been removed. They lived like kings, always indoors. Everyone called the dorm mother Gabby Hayes behind her back. She was in her fifties and smelled of gardenias and cigarette smoke. Her lipstick was thick and cakey, the color of clay flower pots. She prided herself on her hair – it was coppery and resembled scrubbing pads we used in the kitchen. If someone broke the

rules, she would announce to the group at large, "That's not allowed here." The chill in her voice always arrested the deviant.

Life in the Little Girls' House was orderly, neat, regulated.
Before school in the morning we did our chores, young ones
polishing the wooden stairs, older ones carting the laundry in
duffle bags to the laundry building. Some were assigned
kitchen duty, others bathrooms. Everyone, down to the four-
year-olds, had work to do. I was impressed with the efficiency
and equanimity with which work was accomplished. I wrote
letters to our mother, in my experimental loopy left-hand
slant, suggesting job charts on the refrigerator, new systems
we could invent to relieve her of her crushing burden.

There were twenty-three of us. Jan Mary and Suzanne natu-
rally gravitated toward others their age. They slept away from
the oldest girls, in a drafty long hall near Mrs. Hayes's apartment. Our family ties were frayed, and I was genuinely surprised when I met Jan Mary's musing blue eyes in recognition
across the dinner table. She seemed to be saying, How in the
world did we arrive here?

The first day at the new school I was issued a faded blue cotton bloomer for PE. At St. Martin's, PE had meant softball on the
playground. At the new school the locker room was my per-
sonal hell: the body smells, the safety-pinned bras, the stained
slips, the hickeys, the pubic hair growing wild down our
thighs. Sister Michael had always told us not to look at ourselves when we bathed, to be ashamed and vigilant. In the
locker room we girls were elbow to elbow in the narrow aisle
beside the dented pink lockers.

"What is your problem?"

"The F word. That's all he knows these days."

"My mother won't let me."

"Bud's getting a car for his birthday."

Their conversations shimmered around me like a beaded curtain. We couldn't help but see one another – our new breasts, our worn underwear – but the talk kept us on another plane, a place above the locker room, where we could pretend we weren't totally vulnerable, absolutely displayed.

Georgia Cowley, a squat freckled woman, ruled that class with a cruel hand. When I entered the gym for the first time, she waved sharply in my direction and I went over to her.

"Name?"

"Roxanne Miller."

"We're tumbling, Roxanne Miller," she said, writing something on her clipboard. "You ever tumbled?"

"No, ma'am." I looked at the girls casually turning cartwheels, blue blurs, on the hardwood floor. My hope of fading into the wrestling mats for the hour fluttered like a candle in a storm.

"Come out here with me," she said.

I followed her to the sweaty red mat in front of the stage.

"We start with forward rolls. Squat down."

I squatted, glancing desperately around to see if there was someone I could imitate. All motion had wound down, and the girls were gathered in gossip knots, chattering and watching me with slitted eyes. I remember staring at Miss Cowley's gym shoes; there were dried tomato seeds on the toes.

"Tuck your head. Now one foot forward, hands on the mat."

She gave me a little shove to propel me forward. I fell sideways, my pale thigh plopping fishlike on the floor. The girls giggled and hot tears swelled in my head. The seconds on the floor expanded, seemed to go on forever.

"Get up," she said. "Sit over there on the bleachers for a while and watch. You'll get the hang of it." Then she blew her chrome whistle, and the girls lined up to do their forward rolls.

On the bleachers, a Negro girl from Entiat, Nadine, slid next to me, sighing hard. "Got the curse," she said. "I'm sitting out."

"You can sit out?"

"Sure 'nough." She scratched her skinny calf. "You know the secret of cartwheels, Roxanne?"

"No," I said, interested, thinking there might be some secret I could learn from her, some intellectual knowledge that I could translate into body knowledge.

"Catch yourself before you kill yourself," she whispered, as she retied her sneaker. "Catch yo-self." And then she leaped up and turned a few, flinging herself into them with her own peculiar flick of her pink palms above her nappy head.

"Jefferson," Cowley barked. "Sit down and keep quiet."

For the rest of gym period, Nadine and I wrote messages on each other's backs, using our index fingers like pencils through the scratchy blue bloomer blouses.

AT CHRISTMAS we were farmed out. I do not know how these decisions were made. Certainly I don't remember being asked where I would like to go for Christmas. Suzanne went with Mr. and Mrs. Thompson. Jan Mary was taken by Aunt Opal. I went to stay with the family of Darla Reamer, who had been our neighbor for five years. Darla was two years older than I was. When I'd been in fifth grade and Darla in seventh, we rode the school bus together and wrote love notes to one another using a special language we'd developed, a lispish baby talk in writing. Later that year she chose another girl as her best friend and left me miserable. Going to spend Christmas with her and her family, enduring their charity, was like an arduous school assignment I had to survive to attain the next grade. Her mother gave me a Shetland sweater and a jar of Pacquins hand cream. Her father took me out in the wind-crusted snowy field to see his apiary. We went to church, and those brief moments kneeling in the oak pew and at the altar, with its starlike poin-settias, were the only familiarity and peace I experienced. Darla spent many hours on the telephone with Julia, the one who'd taken my place. I was relieved when Mr. Reamer drove me back to Entiat on Christmas night. Many girls were still away and Mrs. Hayes let me stay up late. I drank hot chocolate alone in the dining room and wrote our mother a letter of false cheer and fantasy about the future.

IN THE OLDER GIRLS' sleeping quarters, after lights out, under cover of dark, some girls took turns revealing fears, shames, wishes expressed as truth. When this talk began, their voices shifted from the usual shrill razzmatazz repartee about hairstyles, boys at school, and who'd been caught smoking. They spoke in church whispers.

"My mother tore my lip once. I have five stitches."

"My father's coming to get me on my birthday."

I didn't participate in this round-robin, but instead lay on my stomach, my pillow buckled under my chest, and watched the occasional gossamer thread of headlights on the river road. It seemed there was so much freedom and purpose – a will at work – in night travel. Their talk was sad and low, and I, in my isolation, dreamed of going away, of having the power, the in-estimable power, to say I'm *leaving*. Boys could somehow run away and make it, survive. But everyone knew that a girl's life was over if she ran away from home, or whatever had become home, whatever sheltered her from ruin.

Some nights, if we heard the rush of Mrs. Hayes's shower, we would sing in our thin voices a maudlin song that was pop-ular at the time – "Teen Angel." One night the community of singing gave me courage, and after the song faded, I said, "I saw my mother hit my father with a belt."

As one they sucked in their breath. Then Nadine said, "No wonder your mama in the hospital, girl."

And the others laughed, a false, tentative snicker. I hated Nadine at that moment and felt heartbroken in my hate. I'd always tried to be nice to her, because our mother had said they were just like everyone else inside.

On Valentine's Day, we received a crumpled package wrapped in a brown grocery sack and tied with butcher twine. Inside was a cellophane bag of hard candy hearts stamped BE MINE and I LOVE YOU. Our mother had enclosed three penny valentines and on mine she wrote, "I'm home now with Laura Jean and Christopher. See you soon." She was home! I'd given up on mail from her, but I'd kept writing. I tried to imagine her there with Christopher and the baby, without me to help her, and the thought made me feel invisible, unnecessary in the world. Don't think about it, I said to myself, and I began then the habit of blocking my thoughts with that simple chant. *Don't think about it.*

IN APRIL we were allowed to go home for a weekend.

"Your neighbor's here," Mrs. Hayes whispered in my ear, early that Saturday morning. "Help your sisters dress. I'll give him a tour while he's waiting."

I had a great deal to be excited about: seeing Christopher, going to our old church, being with our mother. Our mother. Her life without me was a puzzle, with crucial pieces missing. I had high hopes about going home. Our mother was well; everyone – Mrs. Hayes, Mr. Reamer – said so.

We met him by his pickup truck. His khakis were spattered with pastel paint; he said he'd been painting his bee boxes. We fell into silence on the drive home. The thought surfaced, like the devil's tempting forefinger, that though we were only an hour's drive from our mother, we hadn't seen her since that morning in December when we went to school not knowing life would be irrevocably changed by the time we returned home. Did she know that morning that she wouldn't see us for four months?

Spring was alive down in the valley. The daffodil leaves were up along the driveway, though the flowers were still just pale shadows of memory, curled tightly and green. Mr. Reamer parked his pickup truck and sat hunched, arms folded across the steering wheel, waiting for us to get out.

We were all shy, bashful, and I hung back, urging Jan Mary and Suzanne forward with little pushes on their shoulder blades.

Jan Mary flinched and said meanly, "Don't push."

"Don't spoil it now," I said.

And we three walked forward in a solemn row down the gravel drive toward the house. We wore our next-best dresses. Mine was a taffeta plaid with a smocked bodice and a sash, and I'd worn my cream-colored knee highs, saving my one pair of nylons for Sunday morning. I hadn't wanted to go home in nylons – they were a new addition to my sock drawer and I was afraid our mother would say I was growing up too fast. The house looked the same, sagging at the roof corners, the gray paint blistering along the bottom of the door. It was a sunny day. Darla Reamer's cocker spaniel came yapping out the drive, flipping and bouncing the way cockers do. As we drew near the house, I saw that Darla was sitting with our mother in that small patch of grass in front of the house. Someone had put a wooden cable spool there for a table, and Darla and Mother sat near each other in lawn chairs. Darla was painting Mother's fingernails.

"Here come my girls," Mother said, waving her free hand.

Music was on inside the house and we could hear it through the open window: *you made me love you.* I didn't know what to do with Darla there. I'd imagined our mother embracing us, welcoming us, with significance. My heart shrank in disappointment, a rancid feeling, everything going sour at once. Suzanne, being only four, went right up to our mother and slipped her little arms around her neck and kissed her cheek. Jan Mary said, "Will you do mine, too, Darla?"

Laura Jean started crying from somewhere in the house. Mother, startled, rose partway from her chair and then sank back, waving her wet fingernails and looking helplessly at Darla. There was a raw, clean smell about the yard, like cornsilk when you go outside to shuck corn in the summer dusk. Darla looked older, in a straight linen skirt with a kick pleat in the back. She had on slim flats and tan-tinted nylons. Her hair was in a French roll.

"I'll get her," Darla said, and she went in the house, letting the screen door slam. Suzanne was close on her heels.

Mother pulled me near, her arm around my waist. "How's my big girl?" she asked. She'd had her black hair frizzed in a permanent wave and her nails were painted fire-engine red. With one hand she shook a Lucky from the pack on the table. A glass of whiskey and melting ice was on the ground beside her chair. Her knuckles looked pink, but the cuts and splits were healed.

"Fine," I said.

"Darla's been helping me," she said.

I held my breath to keep from crying.

I felt exhausted, not the clean exhaustion of after-dark softball but a kind of weariness; I was worn out with the knowledge that life would be different, but not in the way I had imagined or hoped. I didn't want to forgive her for being the way she was, but you have to forgive your mother. She searched my eyes and tried to make some long-ago connection, sweet scrutiny, perhaps the way she'd looked at me when I was a new baby, her first baby. I looked away. Jan Mary gnawed delicately at her cuticles. Christopher came around the corner of the house swinging his Mickey Mantle bat, his leather mitt looped on his belt. The new spring leaves were so bright they hurt my eyes.

Lessons in Joy

BEAU CALLED collect from Belize City on a sleepy Monday morning. Alice fumbled the receiver, said, yes, yes.

"Gordie's van's broken down," he said. "We're stuck here for a few days." A pause. Wherever he was, Alice could hear the rackety belch of a truck or bus, muted reggae, and a hawker – selling what, she wondered, wanting to be there herself, on a foreign street. "You said to call collect."

"That's fine."

"Were you sleeping?"

"I'm in a different time zone."

"I'm sorry."

"It's okay." She cleared her throat. "Really. I have to get up soon anyway." A dollar a minute okay, she thought. There was a lag between his spoken words and the transmission of them, so that they were interrupting one another. Still, she half-anticipated that he must have something important to say. Perhaps, When are you coming back?

She said, "Who's that hollering?"

"Some guy with a tub of lobsters."

She tried to picture him: his home-cut curly hair under a red kerchief, his knees. For Christ's sake, she thought, I'm gaga over his knees. They talked about the weather, they talked about the 49ers, they talked about the dog dying at their favorite saloon, Mama Jane's Rum & Poker Paradise. He said they were going out to the beach to play Frisbee. He never went anywhere without his Frisbee.

Then, "I better go. It's expensive."

"It's okay."

"Are you all right?"

"Uh-huh," Alice stressed. "I'm over culture shock."

"Gordie's waiting, Alice. It's great to hear your voice."

And that was it. She was left holding the receiver, the night still there outside her window, opaque as their conversation. Long distance was the tease of the century, she thought, the empty calories of romance. Her fingers ached from squeezing the phone so hard.

Alice Waverly's weakness was younger men. She'd learned this phrase from an old rockabilly tune on the jukebox in a Chinese restaurant she'd frequented back in Dillon. Except the singer was an old man who said, with a little leer in his voice, "Young girls is my weakness." That's me, she'd recognized, feeling wicked and ashamed, but incorrigible. She liked their spunk, their vulnerability, their childish delight in all things ordinary, hence, sacred: moonlight, puns, raisins in curry, little kids. She liked the way they shivered when you touched them certain ways. They had thin histories and few regrets; that kept them in the present, full bloom now. She liked, too, that she didn't have to be responsible to them somewhere down the crazy river, as another song went. They weren't inquisitive; they didn't collect your fears and longings and hold you hostage; they were easy to leave.

The last one had been Beau. She'd met him at a Peace Corps party near Mango Creek. They had stayed together one month, a month of late-night talks, beach outings, bike rides, daytime lovemaking – the light always pastel through the tattered curtains, the green smooth coconuts just out of reach on the palm tree. Right before Alice had planned to vagabond north, toward the States, they were gripped with the merest beginning of love, something like the first day of coming down with the flu, in spite of themselves. He'd surprised her with the strength of his affection, though she didn't think that had that much to do with her. He was twenty-eight and had love in him waiting to be tapped. Alice had thought she could leave Beau behind. But they'd exchanged a few letters – letters deceptive in their lightness. Much went unsaid, nearly everything. The less he asked, the more she wondered. Mostly she wondered what the letters meant; they were so skeletal; they seemed like the leftover bones of a fine meal.

Now Alice thought of herself as passing through California, though she'd been in Quincy for two months, clerking and baking at a natural foods store. California's not my cup of tea, she'd said to Trina, who owned the store. What scared her were gang wars and toxic yellowy smog and earthquakes. But Quincy was small-town, with one cappuccino bar, no L. A. Times, no chain stores, and high country hiking nearby. Before that she'd been in San Francisco for two weeks with a roommate from years ago, and before that she'd been in Tucson where Matt, her nineteen-year-old son, was studying engineering. She was on her way home to Dillon, Montana, after eight months traveling on an inheritance too small to use for anything else. In January she'd quit her job and flown to Costa Rica and worked her way back, by bus, from there. This was something she'd always wanted to do, and after her father died – suddenly, of a heart attack, at the dry cleaners, right on the heels of her mother, who'd passed away the summer before – Alice was hounded by a sense of time running out, though she was only forty. Now she felt better, years younger.

She was counting on getting her old job back; it was a hard job, counseling divorced women trying to find work. She'd carried a caseload of fifty clients; she'd known their stories; their new boyfriends' names and foibles; their kids' problems – which ones wet the bed, which ones were on the way to being teenage mothers, which ones had trouble reading. It was a job to make you drink to forget, a job that made you cry some-times, a job that could make you cynical about men, if you were the least bit inclined to be that way. Alice wasn't. She loved men. She'd been married once – to a good man she'd tell you, it just hadn't worked out, she'd been just as bullheaded as he was – and she'd had more affairs of the heart than she cared to remember. Alice had trained the young woman they'd hired to take her place and she didn't think she would last long. She was a greenhorn and had no calluses from rubbing up against life.

Her plan was this: return to Dillon and put her father's house on the market; take her things out of storage, comfort herself with her own things again; apply for jobs; go bird-watching on Red Rock River; wax her skis; enjoy winter com-ing on; wait it out. Oh, yes, she had a plan; she just wasn't ex-cited about the plan. But there were people in Dillon expecting her: a man who taught logic at the college who had been – and might still be – a little sweet on Alice; Georgia, her friend at the library, with whom she skied and drank coffee nudges; and Mrs. Hopper, her father's next-door neighbor, whose apart-ment must seem vacant now without Alice's father and his fusty cigar smoke. In memories, she could hear Mrs. Hopper fussing at him, razzing him, calling him a polecat. She could picture her mother's potting shed, with the clay pots and bags of dirt and peat moss. This saddened her, imagining the absence of her parents. She tried not to think about it. She'd bought a sea-green handwoven rug near Lake Atitlán. She could imagine unfolding that rug in a new apartment, doing yoga stretches on the rug, creating her own pleasing space for whatever might happen next in her life. Whatever.

Out the kitchen window of the store, on Wednesday morning, she saw the yellowing cottonwoods – it was mid-September – and Professor Felder, next door at his stone barbecue pit, slopping starter fluid on a Confederate flag windsock.

She went to the screen door, her hands floury with pie dough. "Whatcha doin', Connie?" she called.

"You probably know where this came from," he said, without looking up. "You've probably seen it around. Goddamn rednecks."

Alice had seen the windsock. It had appeared one day on the porch of a duplex rental three streets away. She hadn't seen the new people, just the windsock and the plywood windmills they'd planted in a row along the crocus bed.

Professor Felder's white hair shone like river water in the morning sun. He had it cut in an old style that had become new, thick and long on top, short around the ears and neck. He'd told her it was prematurely white and had been for fifteen years; he was fifty-five. No grass grew under his feet. He wore Birkenstocks with ragg socks, he had an extensive collection of Blue Note jazz CDs (he'd informed her; she hadn't heard them, because she'd steadfastly weaseled out of visiting him at home), and he jogged twelve miles a week. His doctor had told him not to overdo it if he didn't want to ruin his joints. The Professor – that's what she called him to herself, though he had insisted she call him Connie to his face – was retired from parasitology, a widower. His wife, Carla, had taught junior-high English in Davis for twenty-three years.

"Where'd you get it?" she said.

"I filched it, my dear. Liberated it, as we used to say. In the middle of the night."

Alice laughed. "You're asking for trouble," she said, then she turned back to her pies, all berry – blueberry, blackberry, raspberry. Tart and almost sugar-free.

At the window, her hands gently, gently in the dough again, she watched him as he dropped a lit match on the windsock and stepped back, fists on his hips, grinning at Alice, satisfied. The burning windsock lapped into flames like a magic act, and after the first flames died down, it glowed blue and orange around the edges like one of those fake fireplace logs.

From the front of the store Trina said, "Go light on the white death."

"Yes, love," Alice said. She gritted her teeth and chafed under Trina's bossiness. She remembered something Matt's father used to say: The trouble with hippie desserts is that there's never enough sugar in them.

Trina was at the cash register, pricing licorice bars from Finland. She was recovering from hepatitis she'd caught at a blender drink stand in San Miguel, and that's how Alice had come to be there in Quincy, baking pies and carob chip cookies the size of round tarot cards. Trina and she had traveled together in central Mexico. Trina had come down with hepatitis at home and realized she couldn't keep the business open without good help during her recovery. Alice had shown up in Quincy at the right time, and Alice had a charming way of taking over the chores of others and letting them believe they were doing her a favor. She liked cooking good food, with love; there was service in that, something old-fashioned, almost spiritual. She liked the gleam of eggplant piled in lovely curves; the scent of cardamom and cloves; the sizzle of falafel frying. And of course, she liked the little moans of pleasure from people who ate her food, the appreciative glances.

"Addictions are lurking everywhere," Trina said. "And we don't want to contribute to anyone's addiction."

Give me a break, Alice thought. And then, It's time for us to part company while we still respect one another. She thought about how some music is just right for certain times in your life. You think you'll always love the sha-boom of sock hops, a boy's hand trembling on your hip. You hear the music years later and it's laughable, tinny. Places are like that, too, Alice thought, and the time of Quincy might be over soon.

"Just say no's not good enough," Trina prattled on, "We're talking *physical* addiction here. Remember *Sugar Blues*."

Alice sprinkled a shallow layer of tapioca beads on the bottom crusts in the glass pie plates. She tried to picture somewhere else, someplace soothing, a beach, or an eddy on the Red Rock. Joni Mitchell was on the stereo, singing about parking lots. Alice glanced up and saw the Professor in his backyard, his pants pockets pulled out like rabbits' ears, shrugging in her direction and smiling sheepishly. She laughed out loud; experience had taught her what he wanted: a wedge of free hot pie.

After that, they got busy. People from the courthouse came in for mid-morning coffees and baklava; there was a honey delivery; two young mothers, with five children between them, did a month's shopping – buying up bulk rice and couscous like survivalists – while the children flushed the toilet in the bathroom; the pies baked; Alice made the lunch sandwiches, wrapped them in plastic wrap, too efficient and organized to let Trina get under her skin again.

WHEN THE MAIL CAME, she took a break. With a lemonade and her letters and a slice of pie for the Professor, Alice nudged open the screen door, no-hands, and went out to the picnic table behind the store, under the cottonwood. The table was covered with leaves. She could smell new-cut lumber and fall, a kind of damp and pleasant rotting. Beyond the Professor's backyard, three bow hunters in cammies were target shooting. Insects snapped in the tall dry tansy, a sound like a rubberband being rolled off a newspaper.

The Professor sat down and started in on the pie.

Alice shuffled through the mail. There was Matt's faithful letter – he wrote every three weeks – with a bit of graffiti on the back of the envelope: *Reporter: What do you think of Western Civilization? Mr. Ghandi: I think it would be a good idea!* An Exxon bill. She kept forgetting to tell them she'd cut up her card after the oil spill. A request from Planned Parenthood for a donation. A postcard from Mrs. Hopper. And a letter from Central America. Alice's heart punched her chest a little harder when she saw the return address on the airmail envelope. She was surprised at the response she felt at recognizing his handwriting, a response at once curious, anxious, aroused. It was a visceral response; she felt momentarily weak with lust. Wasn't imagination a curse and a blessing? She thought she could feel his mouth on her nipples just from looking at his handwriting. She wanted to get on her magic carpet and be there.

"Mail galore," the Professor said, wiping his chin with a cottonwood leaf.

"My cup runneth over," Alice said.

He licked the fork and then said, "I'll leave you to read it. But later – I'm going to look at some houses. Would you like to come?"

Alice didn't look up. She tapped the edge of one letter against the tabletop. "Not today."

The Professor wandered away, whistling. He'd left his cotton sweater draped over the bench. The bow hunters were disagreeing about something; their voices rose and they talked over one another. One of them – a short man with a stubby black pony tail – slung his bow testily into the open back of a station wagon. Another one spread a big map on the hood of the car. That's what she longed for – a map, certainty, directions for contouring around dangerous places. A cloud pushed a bluish shadow over the backyard, then over the alley. She read Matt's letter first; the gist of it was that he wanted to "stop out" of school for a semester. She felt shocked by this – he hadn't given her any hint of his intentions when she was in Tucson. She drank half the lemonade, set Matt's letter aside, unfolded, under the lemonade glass. In Beau's letter, there was no gist. It was as though he existed only in that ten minutes during which he wrote the letter – she was privy to what music he had on the boombox as he wrote, the cat's acrobatics, and that was that. A cinematic letter. She could see him but she couldn't know his heart and mind.

Trina opened the back door and wagged her kinky blond head. She had a new perm, stiff as a wig. "They're lined up at the register, Alice," she shouted. "I'm desperate."

Yes, ma'am, Alice thought, scooping up the mail. She felt pinched from all sides and remembered a motto on newsprint that Mrs. Hopper had under a teddy bear magnet on her fridge: If you think things are going pretty well, watch out – adversity is probably just around the corner.

THERE WAS PLENTY of lore about your forties. Jane Fonda on a talk show telling the host, Honey, this is what forty looks like! Ingrid Bergman saying, At forty you get the face you deserve. And Lauren Hutton spelling out your options: After forty you have to choose between your bottom and your face. When asked how it felt to turn forty, Alice would say, It's harder to pretend you're a sweet young thing. She had trained herself to sleep on her back to avoid wrinkling her cheeks and forehead. She lay there long into the night, in her dormer room over the store, with the moon sliding by her cracked window, counting question marks like sheep. She admitted she had been thinking of going back to Belize; Dillon hadn't been looking that good, in spite of all her forced fantasies. But common sense – that strict witch – reminded her that the very things she loved about Beau might break her back in the long run. And now Matt. She had a book of accounts – what she could and could not do in order to be a member in good standing of their family unit, as Matt referred to the two of them. She didn't think she could leave the country if Matt dropped out of school. She'd have to be more responsible in the world – she wasn't sure why. And what would she say to him? She didn't want to be the kind of mother who said, Do as I say, not as I do. Something about the loss of potential passion – and not just Beau, but the person she herself became when she was in Belize, a person at once wise and childlike, empowered and willing to risk – imagining that loss made her throat tighten, made her feel, if not exactly old, at least, ageing.

A small rock pinged against her window.

She went to the window and looked down. A street lamp cast a watery salmon-colored light in the yard; everything looked sharply defined and hyperreal, like the leaves, gravel, hedges, of a model train world. And there was the Professor, in a batter's stance on the picnic table, wearing a periwinkle blue jacket and a plaid cap she'd given him from Panajachel. He rubbernecked up at her and grinned. His skin looked hyperreal, too, sun-roughened, he'd told her, from spending so much time in the Central Valley picking up animal droppings to study.

She lugged open the window, wincing at the metallic screech. "What the hell are you doing?" she said. The night was cool. Alice wore a long cotton nightgown printed with rows of a tiny blue and gray fleurs-de-lis.

"You're beautiful," he declared, not the least bit shy.

"Are you drunk?"

"Bet your bottom dollar I'm not," he said. "Why don't you come out to play?"

Alice glanced up and down the alley, hugging herself. The dense covers – down and flannel – were curled back over the bed, beckoning to her. "It's much too late for that, Connie," she said. "Come back tomorrow. Tomorrow's my day off."

The Professor leaped to the ground. "Do you mean it?"

Alice shooed him away. "Yes, yes, I mean it. Now go. It's getting on toward fall, isn't it? Go home and go to bed." She shut the window and watched him meander away. When he turned once to catch her standing at the window, she pressed herself against the wall where he couldn't see. She smiled in the moon-roiled room, stunned at herself for not realizing until now the Professor's intentions. No way can this be more than a corny moonlight encounter, she thought, timeworn, truly timeworn, but she liked the sound of that, *You're beautiful*.

The Professor wanted to buy an old house and start a bed and breakfast out near the Pacific Crest Trail. "Not your run-of-the-mill B & B," he'd told her. "Streamlined. No Little Bo Peeps staring down from the chifforobes. Only teak. Nothing cutesy."

That Thursday afternoon they wheeled over the winding mountain roads in the Professor's mint-green rehabbed VW Bug, poking around lodges that'd been boarded up with plywood and let go, a cedar-shingled bungalow, an A-frame with a shiny tin roof, all places that people were getting rid of. Maybe they'd found a more glitzy place for vacations, maybe business was bad, maybe families just petered out. "Nothing's really grabbing me," the Professor said. "How about you?"

Alice shook her head. "Not a fixer-upper in the bunch. Not a one with character."

They stopped now and then to look at trees. The Professor knew all about them. Grand fir, black oak, sugar pine. And Alice thought what a solid, happy thing she found that trait in a man, some esoteric knowledge about one aspect of nature. Matt's father had known the birds by song and sight and habit; she still missed that.

By and by, in the twilight, they found themselves at Buck's Lake, at the lodge tavern. And that is how they happened to go dancing. The band was called Pie Face. The Professor could really dance, no getting around that. Alice had known this – they'd danced together at a barn dance on the Fourth of July – but she'd forgotten it. The barn had been dismantled for the barnboard, but the stone foundation and floor were still there, in the cradle of the wide valley with the burning stars overhead. Tipsy and happy, they'd danced until the roosters crowed. The Professor had won half a pig, freezer-wrapped, in a drawing, and the next day he'd invited Alice over for a loin roast, but she hadn't gone. Dancing, he made you look good, led you into steps, slick moves, graceful sways – jitterbug, fox-trot, salsa – you never knew you were capable of.

Later they went laughing out into the foggy night. The roads were inpenetrable with fog, the headlights burrowing back at them.

"It's bad," Alice said, suddenly alert.

The Professor pulled over into the gravel shoulder and stopped. He turned off the headlights and slid the heater lever to high. "Let's wait here a bit," he said.

She stared out the passenger window. "It's a long way to Quincy."

"Patience, my dear, patience. It's a virtue possessed by no men and few women."

"These roads make me nervous. Even in broad daylight."

"Alice. You can't prevent disasters."

Alice did not answer for a minute. She pulled up the cuffs of her white cotton socks and folded them down, almost prissily. Then she said, "You're not talking about the roads, are you?"

"What was in those letters, anyway?"

His aftershave smelled citrusy, orangy. "Nothing," she said. "Nothing I feel like getting into." She dug around in her crocheted purse for hand cream, squeezed a dab from the tube and rubbed it over her hands.

"You're grieving about something."

"Grief's a pretty strong word."

She silenced him with that. He folded his arms and stared out his window. Alice did the same.

Finally he ventured, "How's Matt?"

And then she told him: how Matt wanted to stop out of school; how out of control this made her feel; what retro-rebels his friends were; how they listened to the Doors and Jimi Hendrix and talked about buying land and moving to the country; how she worried that Matt would make the same mistakes she made at his age; that Matt might not listen to her or value what she thought. She didn't mention Beau. She had an inkling that if she talked about him his memory might turn as stale as last week's cornbread.

"What mistakes?"

Alice shrugged. "Dropping out. Breaking rules."

"You haven't turned out so badly."

"You don't know."

As they talked, the fog sailed around the mountain, thinned, grew diaphanous.

"It's better now," Alice said.

The Professor shifted around to face her in the cramped car. The backseat was full of fresh basil he'd picked at an herb farm; he was planning to make his own pesto. The darkness was dense, loaflike. He lifted the hair at her neck, touched her at the nape, his fingers cool and deliberate and gentle.

She hadn't been touched in a while, and she sat there liking it, teetering. For just a few seconds she could have gone either way. Then she thought, This is a real person here; he's courting you or thinking about courting you; you don't want to lead him on; think of the trouble. Then she gingerly eased away and said, "We should go. I have to work in the morning."

The Professor turned on the headlights and pulled onto the blacktop road. "Cows to milk and chickens to feed," he said. "I see. I see."

Coming down the hill past the junior college, Alice said, out of the blue, "I could change my mind. About anything."

"That's what minds are for," the Professor said.

Alice laughed out loud. Something about what he said gave her pause, lifted her out of her brooding.

And right before she hopped out of the car, the Professor said, "Don't leave yet. I mean, Quincy."

"Professor," she blurted, striking a sour note altogether and knowing it, even as she spoke, aiming for teasing at the wrong time, "Why don't you mind your own beeswax?"

He flinched. Then he whispered, surprisingly kindly, "You've got a little killjoy in you, Alice."

She was immediately sorry and irritated; her heart hurt a little from hurting him. But she got out of the car and went inside without setting things right.

In her room, she sat in a wicker chair, staring out the window, with just the seashell night-light glistening low in the room. She was resentful that they'd come far enough to be hurt. That was much too far for safety's sake. *Killjoy.* Was that what she'd become? She could see the teal blue side pocket of her backpack under the bed; she imagined packing. Their last words had made her feel at once inert, weighed down, mapless, yet poised for flight.

WITHOUT SAYING GOODBYE, the Professor went out of town, leaving his yellow porch light burning, his kitchen blinds closed. Mail accumulated in his wooden mailbox. Alice felt a little sadness, like a paper cut that kept getting in the way. She watched for him. Catching herself, startling herself, she realized she knew the purling of a Volkswagen engine and that she was listening, keen for that sound. But then she would remind herself, He's not what you're pining for. She wanted closure, friendly forgiveness.

On Saturday morning Trina said, "Listen to this. Some people never learn." She was standing in front of the community bulletin board, stretching both arms over her head. "'Good company. Non-smoker. Urgently needs ride to Seattle Labor Day weekend. Can drive, share expenses, change tires. It's a matter of love.' Then there's a guy's name and a phone number."

Alice was sweeping the wooden floor. She stopped beside the dried fruit bins. "So?"

"So," Trina said, eyeing her. "It's a little corny, don'tcha think? 'It's a matter of love'?"

"I think it's sweet," Alice said meanly.

"Touchy, aren't we?" Trina said.

Later, after the lunch crowd dawdled away, Alice said to Trina, "Next week's my last week." Quitting felt like opening a window on a stuffy room. She'd quit jobs before and the first few weeks were always wonderful, a heady emancipation from routine.

Matt called over the weekend. "It's just for a semester,

Mom. I need to switch my major. To what, I'm not sure."

"What're you thinking of?"

"Do you think people'll think I'm an airhead? I've changed my mind three times this week."

And Alice knew what to say, encouragingly. "That's what minds are for."

Then Matt asked her how to bake a berry pie; she was happy to tell him everything she knew about it–the tapioca, the fragility of the dough, the way you have to use a hot oven for the first twenty minutes to get a good crust. She hung up feeling as though they'd exchanged unexpected gifts.

The Professor came back on Monday evening. Alice spied on him as he unloaded his belongings. There was a saturated orange sky beyond his car, his pale yellow house. She sipped at two fingers of straight gin diluted with lemon juice and pretended she was watching the sunset. A block away, at the Rialto, teenagers were lining up for the six-thirty show. Next to the Professor's house a man and a woman, in matching Day-Glo helmets, swung their legs in arcs over their mountain bikes, springing into the empty street.

She went over and knocked on his door. She'd practiced saying, in a nice way, that she just wanted to tell him she *was* leaving soon. She didn't know what he would say then, but she thought they might have a cup of herbal tea or a glass of wine. She thought it would all work out.

He opened the door and said, "I found it. I found just the place, Alice. Come in, come in. I've got Polaroids."

She entered his kingdom, his territory. His past was abundant in the house, the accretions of a life explored, travel books and poetry books, masks from Latin America on the kitchen wall, shelves of cookbooks – Moroccan, Italian, Alaskan, Thai – a row of burgundy-colored home-canned cherries, cross-country skis and poles in the corner. The place smelled like the basil, which had been abandoned on the kitchen counter before he went away. Alice thought, I'm supposed to learn something here. On the wall were many photographs of the Professor – at the summits of mountains, in a hammock by some tropical sea, in an inner tube on a river with a redheaded woman.

"That's on the Yuba River," he said, watching her intently.

"And the woman – that's Carla?"

"That's her," he said softly.

"She was pretty."

"Yes. Some people think I should get rid of that picture. But it's a comfort to me." Then, "Look." He took her elbow, led her to the teak kitchen table. The snapshots were laid out in a row between a typewriter and a stack of folded paisley napkins.

The house was made of logs, smoky and aged, with a deep front porch and a row of wind chimes glimmering in the sunlight. A big blue spruce slanted to the right of the porch, away from the house. It looked like a place where babies had been born, where people had fallen in love, where, possibly, people had grown old and died. The stone steps swayed down into the yard invitingly.

"Nice tree," Alice said.

"I thought you'd think so."

"How big is the house?"

"Wait'll you see the kitchen. The kitchen'll knock your socks off."

The Professor stood just behind her, his chin grazing her shoulder as they leaned over the snapshots. He smelled a little like a ponderosa pine. With certainty, he rested his palm on her hip. He was intrepid, willing to try again. Alice thought about Carla dying, then her own death. She strained to imagine the end of everything: Matt's letters, dancing, pie dough, confusion, weather, touch. In a wild leap of mind that made her feel almost as though she'd left her body, she thought, It doesn't really matter who you settle on to love, finally, providing you both deserve it.

Later, she would tell him about her parents dying. And then about Beau. He would whisper, So that's what you're grieving over, and he would read aloud to her a poem that Carla had always liked, a poem about unremembered lads and summer ending. She would want to hear all about Carla, his love for her, what was possible. They would put Stan Turrentine on the CD player and slow dance to saxophone in the living room. He would kiss the vaccination scar on her arm.

But for now, in the very changing of her mind, Alice thought about how they might someday – barring any unforeseen disaster – reminisce about coming this far: the fog at Buck's Lake, shimmying to Pie Face, the barn dance, with the stars like stars you were seeing for the first time, that bright, that extravagant. She saw how you could be longing, yearning, for the woman you were at another place, another time, and still be changing, inexorably, into who you were now. The longing and letting go and becoming weren't separate steps in a life; they happened in the same paradoxical moment.

She turned around and breathed deeply, kissed his cheek.

"No cold shoulder this time?" he bantered.

Smiling, Alice said, "Not if you butter me up."

She wondered what would happen next.

Whatever it was, she thought surely history was in the making.

Aces

KIT, BABY," my mother says, "he's my lover, not my husband."

Red light, I think. Our voices grate against the Montana to Mexico connection. It's like we're talking in a tin can, vacuum-packed. My mother says lover the way she says *Brie*, and husband comes out like *saltine*. She's explaining why she can't ask Dan to front Ruck and me the money to retain a lawyer. I can picture her there in San Miguel, among her geraniums, smoking the Virginia Slims her minister brings her in caseloads from Laredo. She can sit on her patio all day and never see the yoked women hauling well water in molasses cans. I've been to Dan's house, which squats high on a mountainside behind a white-washed wall. She and Dan treated Kevin and me to a trip there when Kevin was just a baby, five years ago. Dan's generosity was more evident when they were first together. Before Ruck. B.R., I've heard my mother say to my brother when she thought I wasn't listening. When she's in a certain mood, time in my life is measured *before Ruck* and *after Ruck*.

"Mother," I start. Then I don't know what to say. I want the money and I'm afraid I'll say the wrong thing and screw up my chances. The pay phone receiver's sticky and dirty. My breath is ashen like the sky. It's twenty below in Bozeman, enemy cold, two days before Thanksgiving. I'm at the phone booth outside the Molly Brown, and smashed paper beer cups litter the gravel parking lot. Chilled rivulets of sweat run under my navy pea jacket. My sneakers have holes in the toes; my pink socks tuft frozen through the holes; my feet ache from the cold.

"This is costing, Katherine."

"Are you getting the drift? We were *busted*."

"How did you get out of jail?"

"This woman. Ruck used to work for her."

"Where's Kevin? Poor thing."

"Kevin's with us." I do not want to tell her the way the local deputy said, "Come on, son," to Kevin and led him away in his pajamas and moon boots in the middle of the night. I do not like to remember the embarrassed half-wave Kevin gave me, ducking his head, as though he'd known all along this might happen. Do you know what you think about when you are suddenly separated from your child by forces beyond your control? I didn't think about the sweet afterbath smell of him or the wilted oxeye daisies I find lined in a row in his room or the proud way he recites nursery rhymes. No. I sat on the bed in my cell, the walls of which were painted a hysterical orange, and thought of every rotten remark I'd ever made in exhaustion or impatience. I tormented myself and hoped to God Kevin was not remembering what I was remembering. He's out of the foster home now and he sticks like glue to Ruck.

"Did he do it?"

She means, is he guilty? "No, Mother. You know Ruck. He had the horse barn all set up with his lab, his inventions. Someone – a Jehovah's Witness or the woman who brings the milk – someone just saw all that stuff and misunderstood."

"Metham – what's it called?"

"Methamphetamine. Like diet pills."

"They used to call it speed."

I do not ask her how she knows this, but I remember the Halcion sleeping pills, little blue dream wheels, I once stole from her medicine cabinet. I do not tell her that it doesn't matter to me whether he's guilty or not. Just as it will not matter to the lawyer as long he has his money and Ruck finds a path of even terrain through the truth and never deviates from it.

"They treated us like dangerous people," I say. This seems to strike just the right note, since she knows we are not dangerous people and deserve better treatment. She's bending my way, like a tree under weight of winter snow.

"Are you in Jardine right now?" I hear her blowing smoke away from the phone, a weary sound.

"No, we're in Bozeman. The feds won't let us go back to the trailer yet. They say they're still sifting the evidence."

"Where're you living?"

"In a friend's garage."

"A garage?"

"It's not so bad. Really. It's insulated. There's a wood stove."

"You're not –"

"Not what?"

"You're not sleeping on the floor, are you?"

"Ruck built a loft. Sort of a platform."

She sighs. "What about legal aid? They have that there, don't they?"

"We tried that," I say. "It was no go." Too corrupt for legal aid, I think.

"Give me your number."

"I'm at a pay phone. Ellen can't afford a phone yet."

"Call me again on Thanksgiving," she says. "I'll see what I can do."

"Thank you, Mother," I say. My mooching voice fills me with self-loathing. It's chronic, whenever I speak with her. Thirty-four seems too old to be calling collect, to be asking for money.

"Kit, dear," she says, just before we hang up, "take care."

And for a split second her voice brings tears to my eyes, but that is my response to my own life, not my response to her.

JARDINE, MONTANA, is not a place I ever thought I'd end up.

I went to university at UC–Santa Cruz for two years, had a surfer boyfriend, and took weekend trips with my girlfriends to the Napa Valley, where we'd drink our way from winery to winery in a maroon '65 Impala. We still liked to listen to Motown. This was in 1971, a time when I thought I would – could – be somebody. I wanted to be in advertising or journalism.

But a woman does not find out who she'll be or what life will be like until she has a child. And for most women, having a child is like having all the windows in your house painted shut forever. Liberty is my oldest – thirteen. She lives in Pocatello with her Dad, who's been through several reincarnations – surfer, computer repairman, snowplow driver. Liberty was pure accident, as I believe so many babies are, even now. When I look back on those times, I do not think I made too many conscious decisions about sex; I was wild and only wanted experience; I did not think ahead.

Liberty is a teenager who knows what she needs to know – about IUD's, about diaphragms. She and her friends call them 'phragms. We talk about these things when she comes to visit in the summer. She can say blow job with the the same ease I might have said ice cream cone when I was her age. So far it's all talk, no action. I hope she stays a girl for a few more years, keeps her life for her very own as long as she can.

That was the time of the Big Split between mother and me – when I was pregnant with Liberty. There was no more school, no more surfer boyfriend. I found a job in a bookstore, sold my car to save for the hospital bills, bicycled all over town, and had some notion about baby and me against the world. There were abortions then, but I couldn't bring myself to make the decision, to take control.

I didn't have much money, Liberty was colicky, I had to apply for food stamps, and we lived in a studio apartment where I had to beg the landlord for more heat. The first year of Liberty's life I probably saw the ocean twice; I realized the ocean was not that important to me anymore.

We moved around some after that, to Mendocino, to Klamath Falls, to the Okanogan Valley in central Washington, always looking for a place to be where we could relax, hide out, live cheap. Then Kevin came along when Liberty was seven, conceived in a burst of craziness one weekend when I couldn't stand my four walls anymore. I can't remember his father's name; I had my tubes tied on the delivery table.

Ruck and I met right after that and Ruck babied Kevin like he was his own. I think I loved him for that. There are so many men who won't touch you with a ten foot pole if you have children. I had that handicap – the kids – and Ruck's was an artificial leg. He'd lost his own in a car accident.

We moved to Jardine because Ruck had a friend who'd abandoned this paid-for trailer up there and it sounded good – free rent at the end of the road, with a garden plot, and the mountains like a bulwark against the outside world. We'd given up on getting anywhere, having credit cards, owning anything besides our pickup and chain saw. We wanted to survive with as few hassles as possible. Sometimes I try to remember when it was that I ran out of aces. I think it happened a long time ago, in Santa Cruz, and I just realized it when we were busted.

THE NEXT MORNING Kevin's squirmed down to the bottom of the queen-size futon we're all sleeping on. He's tickling my feet. I'm not very ticklish, but I pretend to be. When I squeal, he giggles. Ruck's breath is warm against my cheek. Sunlight glazes the aluminum strips of insulation between the studs.

"Wuck," Kevin says, suddenly sitting up and shivering, "I want to watch cawtoons." His white-blond hair is cut in a burr all over except for a six-inch rat tail curling on the nape of his smooth neck.

"Rrrr," Ruck says, his palm on my hip.

"Oh, yeah," Kevin says. "Rrrr . . . Wuck."

Ruck kisses my shoulder and switches on the radio. "Cartoons coming right up." He hops out of bed, his sweatpants loose and floppy below his stump. He slips Kevin's jacket over his PJs. "You stay here," Ruck says to me. "I'll set him up inside with Darcy and the VCR. Be back pronto." Darcy is Ellen's little girl. We're staying in Ellen's garage.

Ruck puts on his single Sorel, pushes Kevin's moon boots on over his bare feet and lifts him down to the concrete floor. Then they're out the door, Ruck with one crutch, their voices trailing away, while I'm still snuggled under the flannel sheets and blankets, listening to the Top 40 station. I push away the thought of the garage and concentrate on the embroidery on the top quilt, a flowery line of worn feather stitches, somehow more valuable to me, prettier, because they're old.

Within minutes, Ellen's at the door. She sticks her head inside and says, "Rise and shine, girl. Blueberry muffins are in the oven." Ellen's a morning person. She just got off welfare with a graveyard shift at a Minimart. When we're waking up, she's unwinding from her job, but she's still a morning person.

"Ruck was coming back," I say.

"No longer. I seduced him with those muffins." She cackles.

Inside, it's festive. Ellen's current boyfriend, Glen, is lighting a small marble pipe of hash and its sharp, musty smell hits me first. The kitchen's warm and cozy. A long strand of red chilies hangs over the stove, souvenir of Ellen's summer trip to visit her folks in Socorro. Darcy and Kevin are lounging in front of the television in the living room, separated from the kitchen by only a knee-high bookcase. Ellen's smoking a black cigarette and lip-synching "Cary," which is playing on the radio. She's glossed her lips with shiny magenta. Six people in the house and we're crowded. For a brief inner moment, I'm in California when I hear that song, and my life is still ahead of me, spanning open like a fan you might buy at Pier 1, something foreign and exotic.

Then Kevin says, "Mom, Darcy says Big Bird's a jerk."

We all laugh. That annoys Kevin, but he turns back to the television.

On my way to the bathroom, I squeeze behind Ruck's chair and he reaches out and pats my calf. He and Glen are talking about hash. They remind me of my mother and Dan talking about their wines; after a while in these conversations you realize you've heard it all before. When I come out of the bathroom, the muffins are on the table.

"Real butter, babycakes," Ellen says to me.

Coffee steams in the mugs. Ellen's opened the back door a few inches to get rid of the hash smoke.

Just as I'm breaking open a muffin, there's a knock at the front door. The grown-ups raise their eyes to one another and

Kevin runs over to Ruck. Glen opens the back door wide and the frigid breeze sweeps over us. Ellen flaps her hand, signaling him to close it. She goes to the window behind the television and looks out on the front steps.

"Sally Ann," she says to us.

She opens the door and it's a Salvation Army officer carrying a wicker basket of food. His uniform is royal blue, the elbows and knees shiny from being pressed.

"I'm looking for Katherine Ruckerson," he says, rocking back and forth, toe to heel. His face is a pale slab of authority.

"That's me," I say, spilling my coffee.

"What does he want?" Kevin says to Ruck. Glen has disappeared into the bathroom.

The Sally Ann officer steps inside and Ellen closes the door and folds her arms across her chest and waits beside the door, kind of smirky. His entry into the house changes everything. When someone like that – a social worker or police officer, whoever – comes into your home, you all at once see your house, your kids, the way they might. Kevin's bare feet on the cool linoleum, Darcy's hair ratty, the ashtray full of butts, the cracked window repaired with cardboard and duct tape. Certainly whatever vitality the morning might have had gets let like blood.

I go over to the coffee table. "I'm Kit Ruckerson."

"I'm Captain Cripe," he says. "This is your food basket from the Salvation Army."

"Thanks," I say, taking the basket and setting it on the coffee table.

"Is he a policeman?" Kevin says to Ruck.

The Nylons come on the radio.

"This is a food basket for four. My information stated that you have two children. Is that correct?" His watery blue eyes meet mine.

"I have another child, but she lives in Pocatello."

"Oh, dear," he says. I can see him eyeing the food in the basket, trying to decide what to do. Should he take back the canned spinach or the day-old coffeecake?

I look at Ellen and she rolls her eyes. I am grateful for her. Behind me I can hear Ruck hopping to the sink. He turns on the tap.

"Well," Captain Cripe says, "Have a Happy Thanksgiving." This reminds me of the way my brother in New York always signs his letters "Happy Trails," as though he thinks I'm Dale Evans in Montana.

Ellen opens the door and he waddles out. We crack up when she shuts the door.

"At least," Ruck says, plopping back into his chair, "it's not like the old days when you went to them for a meal and they'd make you drag the 'Old Rugged Cross' around before you could eat."

"At least," Glen says, flinging his long gray ponytail over one shoulder. He picks up a wooden match and uses it to scrape the inside of the pipe bowl.

"Paramilitary, aren't they?" Ellen says, patting Ruck's shoulder as she returns to the table.

"It's a turkey, Mom," Kevin says, pawing through the basket.

"A big bird," Darcy shoots at him.

Our muffins are cold, the sun's blocked by a gauzy cloud, and Ruck hasn't shaved in days. He has more gray now than he did a month ago, and there's a frown line between his eyebrows, a groove he must be cultivating. The things that make us happy are like Cracker Jack toys: Ellen's new job, the gram of hash, songs on the radio. I pour my cold coffee back into the pot and turn the gas up and stare out the window. I try to imagine what I'll be doing this time next year if Ruck's in prison. Nothing comes immediately to mind. The holidays all seem like rituals made for other people, people who have some refuge in the world, some margin of safety, who've never seen the inside of a welfare office or the lust in the eyes of an arresting officer.

Ellen laughs. "He sure took the fucking wind right out of our sails."

SPEED'S NOT a substance to mess around with. Rumor has it that it makes men impotent and women bitchy. I don't think many people do it anymore. I tried it once and I know what homemade speed looks like before it's crystallized: gooey and gray, the texture of Sterno fuel or peanut butter. I never knew what Ruck was doing in the horse barn. He was home, he was affectionate, he spoke to Kevin with respect. That was enough for me. But speed, sweet Jesus, speed.

The time I ate that speed was with Casey, an old boyfriend of mine, who came to see me one June when I was thinning apples in Brewster, Washington, near the Columbia River. I remember we used to catch carp in that river and cook them up with plenty of curry to cover the trash taste. And I remember Liberty had gone to see her dad, and Kevin wasn't born yet. I can remember all this as though it were yesterday – even the songs on the jukebox at the Bohemian Tavern. I guess you can consider yourself fortunate if some of the events in your life take on the sheen of a movie, that romance sheen, when trees are in bloom, light's gold on the water, and you look in the mirror and know you look the best you ever will. That summer was like that for me.

I had worked for nine days straight, thinning the little green reds and golds from the trees of a man named Cooper, who provided a trailer and some cabins for his workers. Every year I'd ever been there, he offered the women extra money – fifty cents more a tree – if they would work topless. I never did, but it's possible I never did just because the price wasn't high enough. After nine days, I woke up thinking, Today's my day off. I dressed up in an old forties church dress, blue rayon with padded shoulders, painted my toenails a color called Sea-Lily, which shimmered like the inside of a seashell, and thought about hitching into town to the Bo for lunch.

I heard a horn toot and when I looked out the window, there was Casey in a little green sports car with rusty fenders. He doffed his cap and said, "Hi, sugarpie," just as though it hadn't been three years since we'd last met. Casey is the kind of man you can have a good time with for a night or two, if you're in the mood to strain your capacity for excess.

We bought a fifth of Cuervo Gold and headed over to Chelan, where he had a connection to buy the speed. We rolled over the river highway, feeling like we owned it, listening to the Dead's "Mars Hotel" and catching up, gossiping about every old hippie we knew between Spokane and Belling-ham. Casey was a shameless gossip.

In Chelan, I waited in the car outside a ma-and-pa grocery while Casey went in and made his deal. I could see the long lake, and the carloads of tourists lined up to take the ferry ride into the glacial heart of the Cascades. I remember I imagined what it might be like to live there in Chelan, on the edge of the wilderness. I liked the thought. This was not unusual for me in those days to think of moving. Moving's something you can do a lot of when you're young; you can kiss your friends good-bye and not look back. When you're older moving takes its toll – it's a kind of death to give up all you've known and start all over somewhere else. But then I could daydream, I could picture it. I wanted to go to brunch in the old white clapboard hotel there, on a Sunday morning. I thought that would be the ulti-mate in elegance.

After Casey came out, we went over to his friend's place,

near the lake, and we stayed there late into the night, eating speed with a knife blade from a sheet of aluminum foil, drinking the tequila, and when that ran out, we walked out for beer. We talked and talked. It seemed we could remember every tiny detail of every meal we'd ever eaten, every argument we'd ever had, every relationship we'd ever been in. We shared the most forgettable details of our childhoods, my Dan River dresses with the sashes in back, his obsession with Sherlock Holmes. We told the true stories of the lovers we'd had before one another, including all the parts we'd left out before, out of discretion or fear. And all the while, there in that Chelan apartment, over a paint store, we listened to the country station on the radio, which was so unlike us, but the music seemed to fit that night: Kitty Wells and Bob Wills and Patsy Cline. I remember Casey saying, "She's *so* sexy," when Patsy Cline sang "Crazy." And the next day, I really didn't care that things seemed a little raw around the edges. I was happy in a way, happy to have talked myself out, to someone I could trust, in Lake Chelan, where nobody knew who I was and the very air seemed a precious cold blue from the firs, the deep lake.

THE NEXT DAY we do Thanksgiving: cook and bake and eat and watch the Christmas parade with Kevin and Darcy. Ruck and Glen go out several times, and each time they return they seem a little more wasted. "It's a holiday, baby," Ruck says, when I give him an evil look. In between the sweet potatoes and the parade and the time Ruck and I make love in the bathroom, I keep going out to call my mother. My whole day revolves around making that connection. Each time, a butchy high-tech voice says that all circuits are busy. Around seven that night, snow begins falling in lacy ellipses, and I decide not to go out anymore.

On Friday, it's a piece of cake. The call goes right through.

"Kit," she says, and right away I hear that she's swallowing tears. "We just can't."

We. There's static on the line behind a shadow conversation, a man saying, "I'll meet you in Butte. At Denny's. We'll take it from there." Even at this distance, I recognize the optimism in his voice and I wish I were talking to him, someone upbeat, someone with solutions.

"You can't."

"But Kit. I have an idea."

No ideas, I think. We need money.

"I could send you that brooch. Grandma's brooch. You could pawn it."

I'm standing at the phone booth behind the Safeway; the heavy grease smell from the deli hangs in the air. There's a man with a bedroll and an army surplus pack, opening the lid to the brown Dumpster. The snow has stopped and the sky is a pale winter blue, like old jeans. I can picture Dan at his rolltop desk writing checks, and I wonder why he can't just write one for me, why he wants to make it difficult for her, why she has to cry and offer me the brooch. Which is probably worth about three hundred dollars anyway.

"Don't do it, Mother," I say.

"Why not?"

"It's not enough anyway."

"It could get you started. You could get it back from the pawn shop when your ship comes in." She giggles.

I want to say, we are marooned on a desert island, there is no fresh water, there are no fucking ships. But in her giggle there is more desperation than I am feeling.

"It would take too long," I say, improvising a response. "To mail it, hock it. We need the money this week."

"What will you do?" she whispers. She's afraid.

"I think we'll sell the truck," I say.

That makes her feel better and, in truth, it makes me feel better, too, knowing that selling the truck is an option, and that if we do, we'll consider ourselves really on the bottom, two people without a vehicle in winter, and that that will probably be the very worst time and improvements are bound to happen after that. I promise to call again in two weeks and we hang up.

I walk down to the courthouse to see the social worker I've been assigned. There's not much traffic; the snow is still pure and untrammeled on the sidewalk. I remember Jardine and wonder if we'll ever call it home again. On a day like this in Jardine, I might have strapped on my beat-up cross-country skis and glided down to town, to Gardiner, where my friend Louisa and I would drink drafts at the Blue Goose and complain about our lives in a good-natured way. Almost always we would go out at dusk, across the potholed street to where the park begins, and we'd listen to the elk cows calling, singing, the way they do. Then she'd have driven me home, five miles into the mountains. I liked going downhill and not having to work my way back up.

At the courthouse, there is one receptionist for all the welfare workers. She is young, around twenty-two, I guess, with a polished made-up face, no smiles, and she keeps herself removed, at a distance, as though she might catch a disease from the people who pass through the door asking for help.

"Did you have a good holiday?" I say, just to put her on the spot, force a reply.

"Yes, thank you," she says, her eyes scanning the appointment book. "Have a seat in the waiting room."

The waiting room is a dull place, with old copies of *Family Circle* and *Redbook*, posters about nutrition, and a laundry basket of broken toys, fire trucks without wheels, dolls without eyes. I count the change in the bottom of my purse and consider buying a bag of Bugler and some rolling papers. Smoking's a crutch I pick up in times of crisis.

My worker comes to the door and invites me into her cubbyhole. She's a big woman, with hair the color of old brass doorknobs; she wears papier-mâché jewelry in the shape of animals – whales, herons, grizzly bears.

When she asks me if Ruck has found a job, I say, out of the blue, "I wonder why I ended up with a man who's handicapped?"

She looks up from her triplicate forms and says, "They're all handicapped, Kit. His just shows." And I see that she has been crying recently, and for a long time. Her eyes and cheeks are swollen. She's not wearing her fake fingernails and her thumb cuticles are ragged, as though she's bitten them.

I stare out the window and say, "No, not yet. We're both looking."

And I think about what might have happened to her Thanksgiving Day to make her that cynical, that hard. A woman can get hard from hurt if it's repeated often enough, and the hardness can make her say the bitterest things. I haven't been hurt much. It's true I've been in some rough water, but I've never been with a man who called me names or made me cry all night. And even as I tell her about the garage and the food basket from Sally Ann, I am picturing Ruck and Kevin waiting at Ellen's for me, and I can be sure that Ruck is giving Kevin his turkey sandwich for lunch and conning him into drinking a glass of milk. I think of selling the truck, finding the lawyer, going to trial, starting over afterwards, all the slogging months of winter ahead of us as we pick up the pieces. And I think, This is just another one of life's predicaments, worse than some, but not as bad as others. For a few minutes, it's like I'm up on Sacajawea Peak, looking down on all of us, instead of locked in my life like a child in a closet.

Hard Feelings

CAROLINE WALKED down through the princess pine and sword fern to the river and beyond, to the spit. The sun was out and this was the time of afternoon when the sun struck the river. The sun was not out often. She fished through the big pockets of her apron and found her Ray-Bans. Through the sunglasses the cedar trees seemed dark and monstrous, the glaze on the riffles like a photographic negative. She considered this hour hers exclusively. She'd cleaned up after lunch, assembled and measured the ingredients for the bouillabaisse, and baked three loaves of herb bread. The last anglers had flown out at dawn. Will was due back soon, from Vancouver, with two new guests who had started their day at O'Hare in Chicago. The spit ran parallel to the bank with a tongue of shallow water lapping in between. Granite stones studded the bank. Two flat-bottomed riverboats – *Tupelo Honey* and *Chinacat Sunflower* – were moored to a stunted cottonwood.

Caroline tried to remember the last time she had listened to Van Morrison. She pictured a moist summer dusk at a commune near Hagerstown, the women in the sloping yard whipping a bedsheet for a tablecloth over a door-and-sawhorse table, the men smoking together near the woodpile. She and

Will had been on their way to Canada, to a new life on the edge of the wilderness. It was just a dream that had spread like gossip then among people their age. Birch hadn't been weaned; she'd been born needing a father and Will had, for the most part, been that father. Though he'd changed. Or Birch had changed. Will had come into their lives when she was nine months old. They'd had a microbus loaded down with all their belongings and a cashier's check for five thousand dollars, all the fortune in the world.

She sat down in one of the low canvas camp chairs, which were frayed and bleached with the weather. One of the guests had left a *New Yorker* face down on the beach next to a grizzly track. The track was six inches longer than the magazine. It was old; the claw depressions, little moon sickles, still sharp; the edges around the heel crumbling. She peeled away her apron and rolled her culottes high to take advantage of the sun. Her legs were pale and though it was July she still had what Will used to call her winter coat, fine strawberry blond hair that grew in an almost invisible layer from her knees down.

Birch was upriver a few hundred yards, sunning her fourteen-year-old body on a flat black boulder. She didn't have her top on. The week before she'd been caught like this by two anglers, who had politely, silently, backed away, but Will had seen it all from a distance. Caroline took off her Ray-Bans to be sure. Birch sat cross-legged and stroked sunscreen on her shoulders and arms. Her breasts were really *there* this year. Her hair was Caroline's hair: kinky and floating, not quite red. They were both glad of that. The green river pooled behind her boulder and beyond that there was a stretch of white water and above that, dense hemlock and spruce cut the view. She could see only the very highest section of dirty blue glacial ice on one mountain.

Caroline stood up and yelled. "Get dressed. Your Dad'll be

here soon." She had the fear that any day now Birch would simply refuse to do what she asked, that she was losing ground as an authority.

Birch didn't respond, so she yelled louder. She didn't like yelling, but the river noise was always there, its crash and caterwaul buffering bird and animal sounds, human voices. The only louder noises were motors, the outboards, the plane, the pandemonium of the generator late at night.

Caroline heard the plane long before she saw it, the swooping drone of the engine as Will sparred with the mountains' eccentric air currents. Birch stood up on the boulder and tipped her breasts back into the bathing suit top. Caroline drooped back into the chair and imagined what they were seeing from the air: the green slash of the valley, female, fertile, against the bold snowy coast range mountains. She was relieved, keen for a reunion with Will, but the argument they'd had that morning slinked around in her thoughts like a scolded dog at dinnertime.

Will had leaned over his logbook in the thin milky light of the fluorescent beam. It was five-thirty in the morning, not quite day, and Caroline had sat braiding her hair in the center of the sagging bed. She wore faded blue longjohns and there was an oily stain on one knee. They had been arguing, and then there was a lull in the argument. The radio was tuned to the flight weather: winds and ceilings and visibility.

"She's acting like . . . like a chippy," Will had hissed. He didn't look at Caroline when he said this. He scratched something in the logbook with a mechanical pencil.

Surprised, unable to believe he meant it, Caroline had laughed. She'd thought Birch's behavior was a small thing, easily corrected, not worth name-calling.

"I mean it."

"She's my daughter," Caroline said.

One of the departing guests came out on the porch one cabin over. "Zip-a-dee-*doo*-dah." Caroline pictured him: the portly margarine executive from San Jose. He hadn't liked her using real butter.

Then they had talked about the flight breakfast, the leftover coho, the dinner plans.

Finally Will said, "Talk to her, Caroline, or we'll board her down in the village for the rest of the summer. She's a distraction to the guests."

"If she summers down there, so do I."

"What would I do without you?"

"Hire someone."

"Caroline."

"I don't want her down there. The kids're up to no good. The keggers go on all night."

Will shut his logbook and, with military precision, placed his pencil in his chest pocket. He clicked the flashlight and they were in the dawn shadows, softer light, returning Will's face to the way Caroline preferred to see him, still handsome, his hair over his forehead drifting a little silver, the intensity of his nettled eyes hidden by the dark.

"Love," he said. He moved close to her on the bed, conspiratorially. "Speak with her. We're in business here. Can't you do this for me?"

"I'll see," Caroline said. It had been all she could muster.

Chippy. Where had he gotten that? She could imagine some Brits saying it, at a tavern down in the valley over a table gummy with stout. Some shift was taking place, the way eddy lines might change after a bad storm or during spring runoff. What bothered her was that there wasn't a male equivalent for chippy. And deeper than that, she was trying to understand that Will saw Birch as an enemy now. He'd been distant and irritable for a few months.

The plane pounced above the flat water a few hundred yards downstream before splashing down, each pontoon spraying a sunny fan of water over the wings. Will would never land so sloppily. Caroline gathered her apron and the magazine and walked down the spit and through the cottonwoods to the trail.

"A ride to write home about," the first man said. He was the older one, the father, and he wore a fishing vest with blond-colored flies perched on the fly patch. He was ready. His aluminum rod cases clanked as he alighted from the plane. "Hello, hello," he said to Caroline, pumping her hand. "I'm Joe. Joe Regalo." His crusty wedding band pressed into her palm. "This is my son Steve. He's hurt himself already."

Caroline saw the new wood of the crutches through the plane window as Steve struggled with them. He was laughing with Trevor. So Trevor had been piloting; he'd worked for them the summer before.

"What happened?" Caroline said.

"It's nothing," Steve said. "A sprain. I twisted it jogging." He situated the rubber tips of the crutches on a boulder and boosted himself out of the plane.

"No more o' your salty jokes now," Trevor said. "Missus, your good man had to stay in Vancouver." He squatted in the plane and handed Caroline a liter of rye and a long black mesh bag of clean towels. "The provincial office – the licensing office – they wanted him to sign some papers an' the papers weren't ready. He asked me to bring these gentlemen up here and fish with them. A nasty job, for sure," he laughed, "but someone has to do it."

"Welcome, Trevor," Caroline said. "Joe. Steve. Welcome to Silverthorne." She nestled the rye and towels in among the boulders.

"This is Caroline," Trevor said, shoving their tweedy Geoffrey Beene luggage toward her. "She's the best cook west of the Fraser River." He winked at her and when he did the wrinkles around his eye made her think of a child's pinwheel. "Steve here – from the sound of it – is the best cook in Chicago."

"That's quite a claim to fame," Caroline said, settling the wide strap of the carryon over her shoulder.

"This is a paradise," Joe said. With his beefy hands on his wide hips, he surveyed the camp, the river, as though he owned the place, and indeed he does, Caroline thought. He's bought us for the week.

"Help, Mom?"

All eyes turned to Birch on the bank. She wore high-topped Converse sneakers and a long T-shirt over her bathing suit. The T-shirt was printed with the words *The Four Stages of Tequila: you're good-looking, you're rich, you're bullet-proof, you're invisible.*

"Yes, of course," Caroline said. "Pick up some of these bags and take them to the guest cabin. To the porch."

Trevor sat back on his haunches, took off his baseball cap, and wiped the top of his bald head. "Growing like a weed, ain't she, missus?"

"That's the way with children, Trevor."

"She's a beauty," Joe said, after Birch was out of earshot.

"Like mother, like daughter," Trevor said. He hung two pair of hip waders over the wing trusses.

Steve hobbled further down the riverbank and gestured with one crutch to an ouzel. His wrapped ankle worried Caroline a little. His father had laid his rod cases against a log, hitched up his khakis, and followed him, with the self-consciousness city people have their first few days in the bush.

Trevor handed her a small cooler that she knew contained her fresh vegetables, and just as the weight of the cooler shifted from his hands to her arms, he said, "Will said to tell you 'no hard feelings,' dearie."

"Look," Steve shouted. "Bald eagles."

"This one's more of a birder than an angler," Trevor said. "Wait'll you show him the heron."

"Is the dearie from him or you?" Caroline said, smirking compliantly, and she turned, loaded down, and followed Birch to the cabins.

TREVOR HAD BROUGHT the Sunday *Vancouver Sun* and a *Rolling Stone*. Birch lay on her stomach on the braided rug in the main cabin, plundering the fashion ads in the newspaper. The dining table was set, candles lit. The generator battled with their peace of mind and Joe and Steve sipped rye on the red leather sofa. Trevor and Caroline scuttled about the kitchen, separated from the dining area by a long island. The island served as cutting board, bar, lunch counter, bookcase. Caroline's cookbooks were stacked helter-skelter, clippings and notecards straggling in among the pages. Three brass lamps hung along the kitchen wall, their shine waxing and waning with the generator's clatter. It was eight o'clock and still a little light outside.

"Did Will say when we might expect him back?" Caroline said. She was cutting dark pink chunks of smoked salmon.

Trevor tore open a packet of stoned-wheat crackers and dumped them into a breadbasket. "He said he'd try to catch a ride up day after tomorry. With the Dean River crew."

"Where's he staying?"

"With his sister in Kitsilano."

"You go on out and have a drink with them, Trevor. I'll finish up in here."

She watched them from the kitchen, she listened. Steve was brushing dust from the inside of his camera. Joe was the serious one, a salesman. He owned an antique shop and Steve had a bakery above the antique shop. They'd lived in Chicago all their lives, on the thirtieth and forty-fourth floors of the same high-rise. They'd been on the Bow in Alberta last year. "Next year New Zealand," Joe said, raising his drink in toast. "The Tongariro." "Be here now," Steve said. Caroline couldn't believe he said that; it took her back in memory to another time. "I just like to get my ducks in a row," Joe said. They were an odd pair, Joe, the cagey collector of Chippendale furniture, and Steve, the young Deadhead who'd turned his health habits into a business. He talked about whole grains and fiber and Jerry Garcia. He put Caroline in mind of a satyr, with his round bottom and short legs, his corona of curly blond hair.

"How's the ankle, lad?" Trevor said.

"I'm not feeling any pain. After this."

"Do you think this'd look good on me?" Birch asked.

Trevor leaned over her newspaper and said, "You'd look fine in anything, Birch. Say, why don't you come fishing with us tomorry? Like you used to do, you know."

Birch curled upright in one fluid motion, drawing in her dignity, her arms around her calves. "I don't go out anymore, Trevor."

She had on washed-out denim jeans, torn in white shreds at the knees and across one thigh. There was something about her fleshy brown knees that made Caroline think of breasts exposed and she supposed that was the idea, to expose herself, in some acceptable manner.

"Don't you get lonely?" Steve said. "For kids your own age?"

"My parents prefer to have me here," Birch said.

"That doesn't answer my question, silly goose. You play backgammon?"

"Sometimes," Birch said.

"Poker's my game tonight," Joe said. "You'll make a fourth, won't you, Caroline?"

"What're we betting? Pasta?"

"Pennies, just pennies," Trevor said.

Birch walked over to her mother, behind the island, and slipped the shoulder of her T-shirt down and said, "Am I tanning or burning?"

Caroline cut her eyes across to the men, slicing into them, to see what they were seeing. Only Steve had paid attention to Birch's question.

"Trevor tells me," Joe said, "you've had a bit of a bear problem this year, Caroline."

She put her arms around Birch and kissed her cheek, the way she might have when she was a little girl, protectively. They were the same size now. "We haven't seen her in a few weeks, actually."

"This far north they're afraid of us," Trevor said.

"My father has a bear gun," Birch said. "I've never been afraid of bears." She pushed away from Caroline. "I'm famished. Really famished. When do we eat?"

The winey smell of the olive oil, the garlic, swelled Caroline's appetite too. "Help me, sweetie," she said to Birch. And she kept her there behind the island, among the ovens and clay bowls, safe in a familiar ritual.

"TWO SUNNY DAYS in a row. Can we stand it?"

"Someone's asleep at the wheel," Caroline said.

"I read that sunshine makes you – like – horny," Birch said.

"I don't think we have to worry," Caroline said, "up here in the rain forest."

Birch arranged a sleeping bag, unzipped and inside up, on her flat sunning boulder. Caroline set her waterlogged Keds side by side and slipped out of her flannel shirt. She wore her old two-piece: a worn bikini, once white, now yellowing, without much stretch left. Birch's snappy suit was printed with flamingos and watermelon slices. She could have been a model.

Her skin had a luminous quality to it.

Caroline tried to remember if her own skin had ever looked like that. When she was fourteen, sunbathing was not something girls did, not in Baltimore, not in her neighborhood. Caroline had grown up in Baltimore, in a flat over a bridal shop on Eastern Avenue. At that time in her life, what she liked doing most was riding the city bus up York Road to The Senator and basking in its dark art deco splendor to see Kim Novak, Elizabeth Taylor, Natalie Wood. Afterward, she'd read her yellowing copies of Photoplay. She'd counted herself lucky if her skin had broken out only on her forehead where she could hide it with her bangs. Hiding had been a way of life: acne, tampons, your period, hickeys, other girls' secrets, phone calls, your feelings.

"What's he doing down there?" Birch said. She meant Steve.

"Splashing around in the Kikkboat. I think the cold water's good for his ankle."

Trevor and Joe had left early in the morning, after a breakfast of Finnish bread and fruit. They'd taken Tupelo Honey, all the gear the boat would hold, a lunch, and a six-pack of Moosehead. Caroline didn't expect them back until nearly dark. They'd filled an extra can of gas for the outboard and gone upriver. She was counting on a fresh catch for dinner.

"Do you think he's cute?"

"Who?"

Birch wiggled her shoulders against the sleeping bag. "You know. Steve."

"He's way too old for you, love." Caroline slapped away a black fly.

"I know that. I'm just asking."

"I guess so. Let me have some of that sun-screen."

"Sun-screen attracts bears," Steve said. "Did you know that?" He was standing on one crutch at the edge of the woods, among the thimbleberries. With one hand he picked the dusky berries and popped them into his mouth. His Patagonia shorts were the lavender of sunsets, a phenomenon Caroline missed – in the mountains you never get the bright sunsets. "They're especially fond of good-looking women, dipped in sun-screen, french-fried."

Birch giggled.

"We stand forewarned," Caroline said. "How'd you like the Kikkboat?"

"It was more fun than reading ten-year-old National Geographics. But I'm getting bored. I'm not healing fast enough."

"It's a shame," Caroline said. She tried to ignore the fillip of arousal she felt.

"D'you ever make croissants?"

"I don't believe I ever have."

"Would you like to? I feel like baking something."

Caroline came up on her elbows and smiled at him and put on her sunglasses. "What a fine idea. Will loves them. He'll be back tomorrow."

"Those are mergansers," Steve said, pointing to the ducks splattering in an eddy. "Not the prettiest duck in the world."

"Have you ever seen a harlequin?" Birch said, all at once agog.

"Those're beautiful, aren't they?" Steve said. "And wood ducks. Ducks are pretty amazing."

Birch flopped over onto her stomach to face him. "I love birds. For their colors alone. There's so much variety."

Caroline thought, Since when?

STEVE STUMPED INTO the dining room, his Walkman dangling from one hand, music dribbling from the head-phones. He sat on a stool at the counter across from Caroline. She was creaming butter for the chocolate prune cake. It was

late afternoon and Birch was showering in the bathhouse next
to the kitchen. Caroline had started a good fire in the Monarch
to bake the cake and that meant the hot water jacket that fed
the shower was blistering. All systems are go, Caroline thought.
Food, fire, showers. It had taken them a long time – years – to
make Silverthorne function smoothly. Those had been the best
times for her and Will – when they were struggling to pull it all
together. They'd lost that mutual striving toward the virtue of
hard work and good enough luck. It wasn't necessary anymore.

"Listen to this," Steve said. He held one headphone to her
ear, reaching across the counter. His T-shirt was dark under the
arms with sweat and Caroline had the unnerving urge to sniff
him there, the way a kitten might burrow in an underarm.

"Alberta Hunter," Caroline said.

Steve sang along. "I'll be down to get you in a taxi, honey."

"Please be ready 'bout half past eight."

He turned up the volume on the Walkman, but all they
could hear was a staticky bass.

"We need a Walkman built for Siamese twins," he said,
snapping his fingers.

She creamed the butter with gusto. "I want to be there when
the band starts playing."

"I saw her in person," Steve said. "Last year. What a
woman."

"You have a nice life, don't you? The best of both worlds."

"I can't complain. I kid you not – I can't complain."

"You ever hear of the Fabulous Thunderbirds?" Birch said.
She stood outside the screen door, a dewy newborn adolescent swaddled in Caroline's long pink terrycloth robe.

"Stop, stop," Caroline said, clutching her midriff. "I'm
media-starved."

Steve said, "You should come to Chicago for a little R and R." The hoopla of his smile seemed like confetti in the kitchen.

After their fine dinner of fish steaks and baked potatoes and stuffed artichoke hearts, after the story of the day's outing – the stately moose spied working his way up a tender green draw of alder, the catch, the party on horseback setting up camp just a few kilometers upstream – after the dishes and the sweeping, after the generator was turned off and the low lamps lit, after Birch settled herself at the table to write her best girlfriend, inviting her up to the camp for a week, after Trevor and Joe opened the backgammon board, Caroline and Steve wandered out to the porch steps and sat down with their brandies. The moon was still behind the mountain, its indirect light wooly across the clouds moving in. Caroline felt a rush of love, an affection, for their place, their isolated life, the balm of it. The river swooshed along and Steve strained to recognize the siffle of some birds near the porch. Sea weather seemed to be insinuating its way up the fjord, up the valley.

They were dressed warmly, Caroline in her culottes and a heavy wool sweater, Steve in a pale blue pile jacket. He fairly glowed in the night, resting his back against the rough-hewn porch pillar, his drink between his knees. She thought of auras. She thought of drubbing his curly hair with her knuckles and she wondered at its springiness, like a brand-new carpet. She was afraid her thoughts were visible, a tattoo on her forehead.

He was talking about his mother, who was visiting a weight-loss spa in Colorado. She did it every year and every year she lost the same ten pounds. He groaned. His groan had a laugh inside it, at its core, sweet and surprising as the center of a hard candy or a French kiss.

"Catch-and-release," Trevor said, inside the cabin. "That's the best approach with fish *and* women."

"Women can think that way, too," Birch warned him.

"You come fishing with us and show us," Joe said.

"I just might. I just might."

The night was lush around them, moist with the weather change, the trees bending like caftan-dressed nymphs, small creatures rustling in among the bracken fern, the huckleberries.

"You and I, Caroline – "

What was he going to say? How could he possibly see through her, into her, already? *Caroline. Caroline.* She'd forgotten how it felt to hear her name from the mouth of a new man. She felt exposed. She didn't usually sit outside with guests like this, drinking and talking in the dark.

"We're people who always want to sit in the middle. Greedy."

"Doesn't everyone want attention?"

"No. *No, no, no.* Dad, for example – let's take an example at hand – he was furious when we threw a surprise party for his birthday. We had those black balloons. A three-tier carrot cake. He hated it."

"Come to think of it, Will's that way too." What betrayal there was in this simple analysis of her husband. He'd long ago made her swear she'd never talk about him to anyone. She thought he was pathologically private. Though, for the most part she'd kept her promise, not because she didn't need to talk, but because they lived the way they did. *In a pumpkin shell,* she often thought.

"The same people work too hard. They work at play. At everything."

"Serious. They're so serious."

"I saw you in the kitchen – humming, shuffling to your own hums. Soliciting attention from that old goat Trevor."

"That's the way Trevor and I *are*."

"Playful. I like that."

Birch came to the screen door, her fuzz of full hair wiry in the lamplight behind her. She seemed tall and imposing.

"Steve," she said. "Are you going out tomorrow?"

"I think I might," he said.

"Me, too."

Caroline's legs firmed over with goosebumps. A wind blew up the river. The moon was rising, like a sliced turnip over Mount Nusatsum. "I'll keep the home fires burning," she said.

THE NEXT MORNING there was a drizzle, fine north coast mist. The cloud ceiling looked as though you could reach up and touch its baffles. Steve's ankle was swollen again and painful. He decided to remain in camp, and after his third cup of coffee he returned to his cabin. Birch went out with Trevor and Joe.

Caroline lingered in the kitchen, leafing through her cookbooks, which was one of her escapes, a path to daydreaming she could justify. She looked up the recipe for croissants and saw that the weather was not right. She did not think that the Dean River crew would be able to fly in today. She drank jasmine tea and tried not to think about how relieved she was that Will would not be able to fly in; she didn't want to face that yet – why she was relieved. She wondered what he was doing down in Kits, in the glory and fever of the city. She remembered herself there, two months before, prowling through the second-hand stores, eating dim sum with Birch, giggling, teaching her to use chopsticks, buying flowers on the street. On a drizzly day, she longed to be somewhere else. She was quite conscious of Steve in his cabin. She could read, she could write letters, but what she really wanted was to peer again into that intimacy they'd begun the night before, to see if it was still there. It was an old temptation. She remembered the others, three of them in ten years, their faces, their habits – one had called her Carrie, one had wanted her to scratch his back almost to the point of pain – and she remembered the crazy way she'd felt after: buoyant and sensual and sick at heart. The buoyancy trickled away within days; the heartsickness lasted for months. Still, she didn't have solid lines drawn about sex; it was a kind of energy, unpredictable and feral. She only knew she did it when she needed to and the source of that need was murky.

She heated an enameled dishpan of water and went out to the back porch. The floor slanted. Broken rods and old orange kapok life jackets were strewn across one end of the porch. Beyond, the gentle rain saturated the bush, the woods; there was a silvery light over the fir duff in the yard; nearby, thrushes made tiny buzzing noises.

She shaved her legs with Will's razor, in long silky strokes through lime-scented shaving cream. Then she braided her hair at the crazed mirror hanging beside the back door. She'd bathed the night before and shaving her legs had been an afterthought. She pinched her cheeks, settled a sou'wester on her head, pulled on black rubber irrigators and a yellow slicker. The clean towels in a plastic grocery bag were her excuse.

"I thought you'd never come," Steve said. He had a fire going in the little airtight stove.

"Here're your clean towels." She laid the bag on the armchair.

"Have you ever seen sandhill cranes around here?" He was lying on the bed – in khakis and a long-john shirt – looking at a red field guide. There was one kerosene lamp lit, its globe sooty, in need of a cleaning.

"What do they look like?"

"Look here," he said, and he rolled over on his side and flattened the field guide open on the edge of the bed.

Caroline sat down beside him and resisted the temptation to reach out and touch him. His temple was damp and pink. She flung her sou'wester on the floor.

"They're the ones with the red caps."

She leaned over the book. His field glasses were lying on the nightstand, and a pocket watch, and a pipe and a pouch of Captain Black tobacco, and a book of matches from Thai Town on North Clark. She hadn't known that he smoked. She realized there were many things about him she didn't know.

Their hands brushed one another while turning the pages of the bird book. Caroline got up and sat in the chair. They allowed themselves to look into each other's eyes, to hold that, to smile, to affirm each other, silently, mostly with ease.

They talked. Their talk entranced her. It was about the simplest, ordinary things, the pleasures of baking, cranes, their childhoods. They argued about Baltimore. Steve had been there once for a baseball game and he thought it was a boring city. Caroline defended Baltimore, its ethnic neighborhoods, Fell's Point, Pratt Library, and this sudden rearing up, this protection of her childhood memories, took her by surprise. She hadn't thought fondly of Baltimore in a long time.

The aphrodisiac distilled of conversation grew palpable in the cabin, sweet and treacherous, intensified by the rain sealing them away. Steve got up to put another log on the fire. He stopped in front of her, touched her jaw. She looked up.

"You're nice," he said. "And this is a fine way to spend a rainy day."

She went outside to pee. She knew she was putting herself in harm's way, and she loved it, loved being there in harm's way, and at the same time traces of panic needled her heart; she felt pushed onstage partly by circumstance, a somewhat reluctant player, though exuberant, too. She wondered what it would be like to kiss him, to reveal her self to him; she imagined this was the way Birch mused about him, like an erotic emergency, with untried girlish longing. Thank God, she thought, I'm still capable of feeling this way.

She had left him sitting on the edge of the bed, tamping Captain Black into the bowl of his pipe. In her slicker and boots she stepped out into the rain, into the pale greenish light of what had become a downpour. They had a rule that everyone had to use the latrines, but she felt like such an outlaw already, she didn't see that it mattered. She squatted beside the cabin next to a rusty outboard propeller. Her face to the sky and rain, she laughed out loud.

"Caroline. What – are – you – doing?" It was Birch, her fists balled at her side, stiff-armed, puzzled. Her name, coming from her daughter, broke the spell she'd been under. Birch stood about ten meters from Caroline in her Converse sneakers and a long black slicker, her hair dripping and dark and wet against her head.

Caroline said, "There's a bear behind you. Come here." She stood up, jerked up her rugby pants, and grabbed the rusty propeller. She opened one arm to Birch.

"It's just a stupid black bear," Birch said, stalking over to the porch steps near Caroline. "He's been following me." She allowed Caroline to hug her, to push her toward the porch steps. "He didn't even have the good sense to get out of the brush. I was on the trail."

The bear lumbered around the edge of the woods, like a drunken pup. His coat was dirty and streaked with mud, his dumb eyes struggled to see.

Steve came to the door, smoking, with one suspender dangling. "What's all the commotion?"

Birch looked him up and down, coolly assessing him. "It's just a black bear."

Caroline heaved the propeller toward the bear. "Get out. Get out of here."

"Vamoose," Steve yelled.

"*Andale, andale,*" Birch sang out. She giggled.

The bear kinked up his neck as if to complain about the rain, and then he blundered away into the bush, trampling huckleberries as he went. Steve went back inside and left them there on the porch together.

"You're a very brave girl," Caroline said, "to keep walking with that bear nearby."

"I'm not afraid. I get that from you."

Caroline hugged her close. They were both wet and cool.

"From me?"

"Who else?"

"Why'd you walk back, sweetie?"

"I'm sick of this weather." She surveyed the sky. "Dad won't be able to fly in today." she said matter-of-factly.

"I think that's safe to say," Caroline whispered. It was late afternoon and the rain would be driving Trevor and Joe back home soon. She thought they would like to have brandy and chocolate prune cake and a warm fire; the evening stretched ahead, delicious and sure, an evening of her own making. She tried not to think of how unfamiliar Will's face would look to her when he returned. She would prepare for that in due time.

She kissed her daughter's forehead. Her return had cheated and protected Caroline, like all varieties of love do, and she wondered if Birch ever felt that way toward her. She sensed herself moving, clumsily, toward lucid questions, toward the arguments that mattered. Then she said, "Do you ever think being here's not enough for us? Now?"

"All the time," Birch said. Then, "That bear hightailed it out of here." She shivered.

The rain was letting up, and they could hear the rough sound of the outboard, like a grouse in the distance. Caroline posed like a bodybuilder and said, "Want to feel my muscle?"

Birch laughed and squeezed her bicep.

Deep Creek

MY PRINCIPAL called to tell me the bad news just as Kath and I had settled into bed after the long drive from Kamloops. Kath had wanted to watch a rerun of the Simon and Garfunkel concert in Central Park. That was fine with me; she'd brought me a glass of rye whiskey and I was contented just lying beside her, figuring in a half-hearted way how to wing it through my classes the next day.

We'd been on a train for three nights, at the end of Christmas break, always a bleak, sad time – facing the winter without the carrot of the holidays – and the train ride from Toronto had been particularly difficult, with extreme temperatures across the prairies and ice building up on the couplings. Every few hours we would stop in the most frozen empty places and the trainmen would get out and sledgehammer the ice away. The train was running thirteen hours late. People were frantically jubilant, prolonging the holiday – last-ditch drinking in the club car, flirting in the narrow passageways. In three days we'd gotten off twice, once for a blood-chilling windy walk on New Year's Day around the deserted streets of Winnipeg – where the digital thermometer at a bank read minus thirty-four – and once in Banff, where the mountains, the chalets, the bright icicles as thick as lodgepole pine, all this seemed like the setting of a fairy tale, a place that would never change. The conductor warned us to take shallow breaths through our scarves to keep from frostbiting our lungs.

Kath and I had been married three years and our marriage was to last a year after that. We'd been in a trough of misunderstanding for most of the trip, and we'd only just begun to come out of it, a reconciliation forced like an amaryllis by the close confines of a train berth. In Banff, beside the engine's great machinery, with the winter sun setting the color of wine on the snowy mountains, Kath said, "Let's always be good to one another." She had her arm through mine and patted me with plump yellow ski mittens. I agreed, I thought that was a good thing for her to say at that moment. She was contrite and I wanted to be the same, to put behind us all that had been bothering us. At times like that, standing somewhere in the high country, on a journey, cut off from familiarity, it is easy to pretend you can move ahead in life together with only the two of you of any consequence. It is easy to pretend you are not at the mercy of circumstance and the past and the reservoir of misgivings pooled between you.

I answered the phone on the first ring. I recognized my principal's voice – British, well mannered, but intimate – and we had stopped identifying ourselves at the start of telephone calls. "David," he said, "there's been some trouble. Terrible news. I thought you should know before school takes up."

I reached for the remote control near Kath's hand and pressed the mute button. She flung back the covers and barged out of the room, her rayon boxer shorts silky around her thighs. It registered with me how tenuous our truce was. She was irritated by my taking phone calls about school at home or having students over to the house. She liked to keep work separate from our private lives, as though it didn't have everything to do with who we were in our private lives. I believed then, and I still believe, that work that matters is rooted in your heart, like a love that matters. But I didn't say that to Kath. I tried to appease her. It was one of the ways I pruned myself back to keep the daily struggles to a minimum. I'm sure she pruned herself back too, denying things to keep the peace.

Then my principal told me that one of my students, Andrew, was in jail for raping and murdering a little girl. My mind clanged with questions, and denial, but I could not speak. The moment would forever be steeped in the sour brine of all that had gone wrong that year, and I would remember and remember that phone call with a terrible awe. He said it was alcohol-related; he said the little girl was two years old.

I HAD BEEN a teacher for only two months when Andrew came into my classroom, in late October, too far into the semester to ever catch up. He was older than the others by several years, possibly sixteen or so. Part Indian, not as dark as some, strong, well built, he was nearly a man, though I was stronger still. He held his head down evasively, his crow-black hair waving aimlessly over his broad forehead. He had showy dimples when he smiled. I counted it a good day if I could get a direct look from Andrew, a slip of a smile. It became something I worked toward. I let him play his guitar in the back of the room on the sofa if he'd finished his regular work. I gave him special projects: painting the side panels of a bookcase with an Indian design of black and red birds, keeping the art supplies organized. I tried to win him; I thought everyone could be won. I thought I could ignore what I didn't like, praise what I appreciated, and win them. It was my first year teaching.

When the job offer came through, Kath and I had moved to

the Valley sight unseen. We knew, from looking it up in a book at the public library, that we would have to drive three hundred miles on a dirt road to arrive here. It was not an easy year to find a teaching job in British Columbia. In fact, later in the year we would go on strike, for three days, picketing in front of the red brick schoolhouse in the freezing rain, hard put to keep a fire going in the rusted trash barrel out on the main road, and over what? Nothing so important as better working conditions or more money. When things got worse and there were more budget cuts – something we knew was just around the corner – we wanted the right to lay off our colleagues in a fair fashion. That was what the strike was about. We knew layoffs were inevitable; it would have been unconscionable if they – the administration – had been able to pick and choose arbitrarily who would be the first to go. We thought they would pick the ones who taught evolution or human sexuality or Marxism side by side with capitalism. But the strike is not what's on my mind. I'm trying to make sense of earlier events. That came later in the year, when I was worn out with questioning all the high-minded ideals I'd come there with.

The Valley is an isolated place, at the end of the road we liked to say. It had been nearly fished out and logged out, but people hadn't come to terms with that yet. No one wanted to pick up stakes and start all over somewhere else. It was a little paradise, temperate, sixty miles from the ocean up a fjord, with a long growing season. Kath and I talked about having a garden and sometimes after dinner we'd look at seed catalogs and say the names of vegetables as though they were invested with meaning. We liked the sounds of them: rutabaga, summer squash. Kath liked to make practical plans with me, to talk about building a greenhouse or buying a dory. It was her way of insuring our future and I didn't mind that. As it has turned out, she needed to insure that future more than I did; she doubted it more. We weren't the only ones who wanted to live at the end of the road. An uneasy, cooperative clot of people lived in the Valley: native Canadians, back-to-the-landers, immigrants, Jehovah's Witnesses, Mormons. We lived in a cone-shaped handmade house next to the river. The house had thirty-two windows and kitchen cupboards made of custom-milled birch; it was common to see bald eagles from the bedroom.

My life was just beginning to feel like mine again. I'd resisted the Vietnam draft by moving to Canada in 1972. I was the eldest in a troubled family with a depressed mother, a sometimes absent father, a little sister with an orthopedic birth defect, and I had shouldered my share, or some would say more than my share, of responsibility, though I had made my peace with all that and I thought it was true what people said about adversity – that it can make you strong in ways you might never have been without it. *Evader* is a label not easily shed; it's like being called *stupid* or *homely* when you're young. I was nineteen and it was the first time in my life I'd been conscious of having to choose between two bad situations. I left for Toronto and worked my way across the plains and the Rockies to Vancouver. Living that way – as an outlaw, angry and powerless, homeless in a sense, though I always had a place to call home, a roof over my head, the country of Canada was vast and unknown, the mysterious far north, and her names of mountains and rivers and creeks never resonated with me – living that way had taken its toll. I was a stranger and kept myself a stranger and for a long time; a day or a week seemed like only something to endure.

Then I met Kath. Kath was a brash, rough-and-ready, field hockey sort of woman, whose Australian family had moved to Victoria after the last world war. She was exuberant and tall and ruddy-cheeked, quick to tease and flare up in anger, usually just as quick to forgive. She wore her blond hair in a practical Dutch bob – low-maintenance hair, she called it. She taught aerobics classes at the Legion four evenings a week. At that time in our lives Kath would think nothing of lying about the house for hours of a Sunday, in her watch-plaid flannel nightgown and gray wool socks, listening to the BBC and drinking strong tea and making love. Now she's more ambitious; she's going to acupuncture school in Seattle. I haven't heard from her since last Christmas – she sent me a tin of shortbread wedges from a gourmet shop. It has been five years since our divorce was final. Sometimes I come across a snapshot of her – proudly holding a fish she'd caught or sunbathing at the river – and I am still surprised that we are divorced. I did not ever think that this would happen in my life. The thought can cut into me like a snake's rattle on the trail, a shock that can only mean harm. No two ways about it. But I do not throw the snapshots out.

When we were first together, she wasn't ever timid in bed and she liked to talk politics. She could catch and clean fish, though she didn't like being the one to strike them the final blow that would kill them, particularly the big ones, as they wallowed on the sandy bank of the river. I did not like that either. But it made us both feel secure and capable to have a freezer full of salmon steaks, and in the beginning it was good being there with her on the edge of the wilderness. We were still getting to know one another.

OUR TRIP to the States had not been restful or rejuvenating. My mother had had her first heart attack in September, three days before her fifty-fifth birthday. My father had called and said, "Come and have Christmas with your mother. We don't know how she'll be a year from now."

It was only my second time across the border since amnesty. We'd driven a rented Mazda from Toronto to western Maryland, to Deep Creek Lake, where my father had rented a cottage named "The Pines." The cottage had been there since the thirties, built of indigenous stone the color of graham crackers. It had a view of the gray frozen lake and the snowmobiles, zips of yellow and red in an otherwise exsanguine winter landscape. A caretaker had filled a zinc trash can with split chunks of cedar kindling. My father – we all called him Bud – had stocked the kitchen with liters of gin and vodka and bourbon and liqueurs – for the girls and their girl drinks, he said – as well as salamis, rye rolls, crusty loaves of sourdough, tiny boxes of breakfast cereal, sugar cookies.

When we arrived, around noon on Christmas Eve, my mother presided over the oak table in the dining room, in a cobalt blue sweat suit, her thick white hair coarse and in need of a trim; she had before her on the table a short tumbler of bourbon, her Marlboro Lights, matches from the Red Run Inn, her tranquilizers in a plastic prescription container, a pearl rosary, and an old telegram she'd retrieved from a box of family letters.

"So you're home," she said, as though I'd been away for a few months instead of years. This was 1981. She took breathy quick draws on her cigarette. She didn't get up.

The TV was on – some explosive car crash. My father was out shopping. The lights on the tree blinked randomly.

"Goddamn time," said my brother, Larry, getting up to pump my hand. He smoked a cigar. He was twenty-four, a graduate student at College Park, and he looked as though he didn't yet need to shave; he looked that young. "Nice sunglasses," he said. I hardly recognized him. My other brothers and sisters were due to arrive later that night.

I hugged my mother's shoulders, introduced Kath. My

mother compulsively rearranged the matches, the cigarettes, the bourbon, the telegram, the rosary, on the table in front of her. She looked much older and sicker than she had in 1972. Her face was puffy from the drinking, whitish-gray as school paste. It was painful for me to see the damage she'd done to herself. She stared at the knotty pine ceiling.

"What's that telegram?" I said to her, blindly, not really knowing what to say.

"She won't let anyone read it," Larry shrugged.

The telegram was old, tinged brown along the edges.

"There's always bad news," my mother said, in a stern far-away prophet's voice, the same voice she used to use when she'd say "The Democrats always get us into war." She didn't look at anyone when she spoke. She turned sideways in her straight-back chair and I could see that she constantly jiggled one knee.

I went out to the kitchen to pour myself a drink. Kath said she had a craving for orange juice over ice. I thought it was going to be a hard Christmas and I wasn't wrong about that.

THESE ARE the things Kath and I talked about on the drive from Toronto to Deep Creek Lake: the intentions of the people in the Valley, how to handle the gossip about us, the way my job absorbed me, and whether to leave the Valley. "We're not arguing," we each affirmed at least once during the drive. In truth, our talking felt like the labor of oxen yoked together for life, going in the same muddy circle. We were mired in tension.

There had been gossip and quite a bit of it. We were suspect – different – on many counts: we didn't go to church, we didn't have children, we didn't watch much television. We weren't the only people like ourselves in the Valley; we were just the most recent to settle in, latecomers, mysterious fresh targets for the people who talked, the people who liked to while away time speculating.

The most vicious gossip had been about Kath. She had tried to start a women's spirituality circle like the one she'd belonged to in Vancouver. They had met on each full moon to do rituals and chant. It was a kind of benign witchcraft, pure and simple, a kind of paganism. Sometimes they wrote letters for Amnesty International, sometimes they talked about their childhoods, their disillusionment with what they called patriarchal religions. The Valley wasn't ready for this. Kath was shunned by some people; a few women dropped away from her aerobics class, even though they were paid up for six weeks in advance. And then our cleaning woman, Willie Sue Vinton, a pinched-looking, spiteful neighbor, read Kath's dream books and went around the Valley telling people the dreams as though they had really happened. Kath was an avid dreamer; these are night dreams I'm talking about – wishes, fears, erotic encounters with strangers and friends, the unearthing of truth about herself as she sleeps, the dark side brought into the light. She had the habit of writing down her dreams in a school notebook, the kind with a speckled, black-and-white hardboard cover. In the study we shared, she kept a row of these notebooks on the bookshelf. She said she remembered her dreams so well because she didn't poison her system with booze and caffeine, because she stayed "in balance." She felt violated by Willie Sue Vinton. "Never," she screamed at me. "I will never get over this." She'd pointed a fierce finger at me and said, "Don't you dare ask me to get over it."

We began to feel trapped, as winter came on. To make matters worse, Willie Sue kept cleaning for us; it had been an agreement made with the owners of the house, our absentee landlords, who had the house on the market and wanted it in mint condition should a potential buyer drop by. But I had my work, which sustained me marginally. And I had the hope that that would get better; everyone said your first year was the hardest. Kath had more time to brood, and brood she did. Nothing was her fault, though; I know that. She was a woman with too unpredictable a life to ever fit in here, really fit in. Some would contend that everything you need to live and grow is here, in the Valley, if you can give up wanting more. That's the key, giving up wanting more. Loving what is instead of bemoaning what isn't. I thought we should stick it out – focus on the positive, the view of glaciated peaks outside our kitchen window, the good salary I earned, my first-ever decent salary, the summer free – and Kath thought we should leave at the end of the school year.

We finally did quarrel at a Howard Johnson's near the Pennsylvania Turnpike. Kath leaned across the booth table, pushing aside the remains of her chicken pot pie, and said, "You know that kid – Andrew?"

Curt, impatient, and tired, I said, "Yeah? What about him?" It was six in the morning and the roads had been icy. We'd come across cars in dark snowy drifts, their taillights blinking, waiting for tow trucks.

She put her elbows on the table, her hands over her mouth. She opened her hands like shutters and whispered, "He spied on me."

Just then the waitress came by and topped off my coffee.

After that I said, lowering my voice, "What do you mean – he spied on you?" I could tell she thought this was one of her high cards, something she'd been withholding that might make a difference.

She took a sip of tea, then tucked a paper napkin under the cup to soak up the little that had somehow spilled. "When he came over that time. After the storm."

I had hired Andrew to pick up and stack the limbs and twigs littering our yard after a wild and lovely thunderstorm in early November.

"So what happened?"

"I was practicing a new routine in the living room. It was John Cougar and it wasn't going very well – the beat's too slow. I was wearing tights and – "

"What's that got to do with it?"

"I'm just telling you what happened."

"So tell me."

"I was looking for another tape, something bouncier. And when I turned around to begin again, he was there."

"Where?"

"On the little porch off the kitchen."

"What happened then?"

"All I know is this, David – he had the weirdest look in his eye. He gave me the creeps. I said hi – "

"Why'd you say hi if he gave you the creeps?"

"He's your student. I thought you wanted me to be nice to them." She sulked, slumping against the padded bench.

There was a stubbornness taking root in her. And in me, too. Her reasons for eventually leaving were calcifying. From that night on, it seemed, she would cling to how she saw me, to her central complaint about me: my unrelenting idealism, my blindness. I've watched other marriages get played out this way; we make up our minds; we see what we want to see.

"There's something wrong with him," she said. "You'll see. Willie Sue said he shot his mother when he was ten years old."

"Shot his mother?"

"In the arm. He shot his mother in the arm."

I sighed deeply, shook my head. "It's hard to imagine how

much damage must've been done to him to make him do that."

"I was there by myself," Kath said. "He could've hurt me."

I snatched up the check and reached for my wallet. I said, "You keep the doors locked. You hear me?"

WE STAYED at Deep Creek Lake for five days. Being there for Christmas with its attendant dead time, time to mull and ruminate, made me wonder – for the first time – if I'd left for reasons other than the draft. I had trouble looking my mother in the eyes. I wanted to, intended to. I told Kath on the second night that I wanted to open up to my mother, ask her questions that had nagged me for years. And every night before we went to sleep Kath would say, "Did you?" And I would know what she meant. And I'd say, "Not yet."

My father and I were able to talk about certain things, the geography of Canada, the Chicago Cubs, my mother's heart attack. He talked about it as though it were over, done with, a piece of history. No one could confront what she'd become, where she'd been taken by her illnesses, her unhappiness, her trauma, the trauma of a life uncertain and angry. Whenever we didn't know what to say, we'd play with the children, my nieces and nephews; we'd delight in their every smile, every trick.

Two memories rise in sharp relief when I think of that time.

The night before we were to leave, Larry and I went for a walk. We were not quite drunk. The stars were bright, the sky like tumbled stone. I had gone to high school there, in Garrett County, and since that time suburban condos had been built along the lakeshore on tight sixty-foot lots. The sweet smell of fabric softener huffed from the clothes dryer vents of the houses we passed. Larry talked about development, wondered how far it might go before it all collapsed back on itself. We were on a ski path that meandered between the road and the lake, in and out of wooded groves.

He led me down to the lake on a trail slick with cross-country ski tracks. The trees – swaying, whining – were black against the bluish snow. Neither of us wanted to talk about what the other wanted to talk about. I asked him about school: when might his dissertation be finished? what would he do then? He seemed not to care. He said he liked the life of a student; if your bills were late people attributed only the purest motives to you. And he asked me about mother: what did I think of her now? was there nothing we could do to help?

I stamped down the snow beside a log and sat down. The waning moon glimmered, the icy lake's edge creaked nearby. My head ached in a band like a tight hat.

"Do you remember that Bob Dylan concert?" Larry said.

"Vaguely."

He batted some tall woolgrass with his mitten. "I thought we were having the time of our lives. I was only thirteen."

I said, "It wasn't that great."

"We hitched a ride home in the sleet. With those people on their way to Florida from Vermont."

"They had some acid."

"*Exceptionally pure,*" we quoted, in unison. We laughed. That cusp of memory, the same memory, was our point of reunion. It was as close as we could be, a disappointment buried in me like foreign matter left behind by a doctor during surgery, something that would flare up later and cause trouble.

Walking back, we passed a clump of snowmobilers tinkering with their engines. They were dressed in quilted snowsuits, except for the one woman among them – she wore pink nylon ski pants and a heavy Scandinavian sweater. She handed a leather bota bag to one of the men, coaxing, "Get off the runway, sweetie. Have some schnapps."

Larry said, "I've got a joint."

Back at the cottage, we smoked part of the joint outside on the shoveled walkway. We hunched our shoulders, shivering. Then Larry got in his car. He said he was meeting some old high-school pals at Ward's Tavern, in town, a place that still put out a free lunch every day. Some of his friends had worked since junior high at the turkey-processing plant and I always thought Ward's smelled like raw turkey. He did not invite me to come along. This seemed peculiar to me, out of sync, that we would smoke the joint and then part company. I wanted to stay up talking, to push ourselves beyond the limit, to revelation. But I made no move to stop him.

Inside I came upon my wife and my mother talking in the kitchen in the bright sharp lights. I saw them from the darkened living room, where only the pinholes of green and blue and red blinked on the tree. My father had fallen asleep on the sofa. He wore a plaid flannel shirt and even in sleep, snoring, he had his arms folded tightly across his chest. My blood beat wildly, irrigated by the marijuana we'd smoked. I sat down at the table and watched them, listening, dreading every word. I felt nearly ill with that old childhood shame about my mother.

"I don't want them to sleep outside," my mother said.

Kath said, "No one's sleeping outside." Her voice sounded soothing, authoritative in a sweet way, persuasive. I had the sense that they'd been talking for a while.

My mother washed down a pill with 7-Up, her back to me. She abruptly laid her head down on the counter, on her arms, and a bottle of gin fell in the sink and broke.

Kath moved toward her protectively. "Don't hurt yourself," she said.

"Smell that. That's a sentimental smell. Like Kokomo when I was a girl. Like Grandpa Bowler."

"Smells good, doesn't it," Kath said. I didn't think she meant that.

"When I die," my mother said, "if it's in winter, don't bury me then." She ran her hands roughly through her hair, pushing it away from her face.

"We won't do anything you don't want."

My mother felt around on the counter behind her for her Marlboros. "I can't stand to think of that." She lit a cigarette. "I'm waiting to die – that's true enough – but don't bury me in winter."

I felt choked with all the questions I'd wanted to ask my mother and never would. *When you were a girl, what were your dreams? What was it like in the hospital those times? Did you love my father when you married him? Where does it come from – all the ruin?* My mother died three months later, of a second heart attack, in her sleep; she was buried when the ground was just beginning to thaw. We didn't return to Maryland for the funeral, telling ourselves, We saw her right before she died, we were just there. Still beginners at death, we didn't understand that funerals are for the living. "It's all right," Kath had crooned to me as I lay rigid in bed with unexpressed, contained grief. "It's early spring there. It's not winter anymore."

"WHAT'S HAPPENING?" Kath said. She pressed the mute button and the concert volume came up. She perched next to me on the bed, her head tilted toward me, her beautiful bare legs so much there, within my reach. I felt as though I might vomit; the rye burned retchingly in my chest and throat.

I told her what my principal had said about Andrew.

"Jesus fuck," she exhaled. "I knew it."

I roared at her, "You – did not – know – it." The roar shriveled into weeping. My hands shook helplessly. I felt separate from my hands.

"Who're you crying for?" Kath said. "Don't you dare cry for him. He's a monster."

"Kath – please," I said, my arm outstretched. "Don't be at odds with me."

She gripped my hand. "I won't be. I won't be at odds with you," she whispered, her voice hoarse, intense. "But you can't ignore this. That'd be evil. The worst kind of evil."

All the time before I had thought that you pay your dues and, with luck, you might see an end to loss. But that night I knew for certain that each loss in a life is just the next one. Clearly, clearly, I saw the chain of meanness there was in the world, how tough, what labor it was to struggle against that; knowledge like a bad dream or fall knocked the wind out of me. Kath twisted away and stared out the window, her mouth hardened with the desire for revenge, or truth.

The Late Hunt

SOME DAYS Blue wants to get PG. She can't decide if she would rather move to Denver or get PG.

"Air's bad in Denver," Randy says.

Blue says, "But they have more snow."

Big Sky Resort – where Randy works in the winter – has closed down due to lack of snow. He put in his UI application the Friday before the late hunt. The clerk at Job Service gave him a hard time and he just squeaked in under the wire with enough weeks of work to make him eligible. "We'll make it through the winter," Blue assures him, at least once a day, until Randy tells her to stop talking to herself. She brings home eighty-eight dollars and thirty-two cents every Friday from her cashiering job at Poor Isaac's, the downtown newsstand. Randy spends his unemployed days tying flies, watching Phil Donahue, and reading Outside magazine; he talks about buying a llama for pack trips. When Blue comes home, supper's usually on the table; Randy's speciality is elk loin steaks cooked according to Julia Child in red wine and garlic butter.

Blue doesn't want to go hunting. Randy tried to find someone else, with no luck. He has a doe tag that's good for five days on a ranch east of Livingston. His back bothers him and he needs a partner to help with the lifting, the dragging. Blue zealously guards her Sundays, when nothing is scheduled, when she can read the week-old *Denver Post* she scavenges every Saturday night from Isaac's back room. Randy coaxes her into going; they'll leave late in the morning; he'll give her a foot massage when they get home. She packs a Thermos of Montana Gold tea and a chocolate bar, thinking, Maybe we won't get anything.

The interstate is icy, the sky gray and wrinkled as a mussel shell. Randy drives and Blue scans the sides of the freeway ahead for ditched vehicles, prepared to warn Randy in advance about the slippery spots.

"There's an article in last week's *Post*," Blue says, "about the five stages of love."

Randy says, "Would you pour me some tea?" He hands her a blue Minimart mug he's pulled from under his seat. The mug handle is enameled with dried blood from some other hunt. "The fifth stage is cocreation, where you make something together. A book. Or a business. Or a baby," she says, pouring from the metal Thermos. She spills a little when they slide on the ice. Randy is good at recoveries on ice. "A baby, for example."

"Men don't think about love the way women do," Randy says.

The way he says it – decisively, as though closing a window against a storm – lets Blue know the topic is finished so far as he's concerned. Her inner life's becoming a burden, more than she can carry. Changes wake up in her like sow bears in spring and she doesn't understand them all. Years ago, in some tavern, if she'd heard "Honky Tonk Woman," she'd have felt sexy and reckless, like dancing with a stranger and maybe letting him see a little way down her shirt. Now when Randy slips *Get*

Yer Ya-Yahs Out into the tapedeck, she imagines cruel struggles between Mick Jagger and anonymous women who don't know any better. And they always submit to him. Maybe MTV makes her think this way. The song disgusts her, makes her skin crawl, and who can she tell?

Her best friend, Mona, doesn't seem like a best friend because she's married to Tom, Randy's pal. Anything she says to Mona feels like betrayal. The closest she's come to being honest was one night last winter when Randy and Tom were gone all weekend with Search and Rescue, looking for two skiers who were lost in the Bridgers. Mona had spent the night. They drank Liebfraumilch and listened to old forty-fives, records from 1964 Blue keeps stashed in a pink satin heart-shaped candy box. The songs had brought back memories. Eventually, after midnight, they had told one another about their early sexual experiences, from the age of thirteen on, and the talk had been exhilarating, breaking past the polite barriers. But the next day, and ever after, Blue felt embarrassed and sad and ripped off, as though she'd let a piece of herself go with Mona, a piece she'd never retrieve. It felt like snagging a fishing lure on rocks and having to cut it loose. Just when she thought she was going to catch something, she ended up losing something. That was the trouble with confiding in someone – you gave away too much of yourself, and if you didn't watch out, pretty soon you'd have nothing left. Or so Randy had warned her several times in the three years they'd been married.

"Randy sure is a mystery man," Mona had commented to her on more than one occasion, in the privacy of the kitchen as they mixed margaritas or salad dressing. She had a wistful tone in her voice that made Blue think Mona wished she could penetrate that mystery. That scared Blue and made her come on to Randy later in the night, seeing him as she thought Mona did.

"Mick Jagger and what's-her-name – the model, the blond one – they have a baby," she says.

"Mick Jagger's a candy-ass."

"What's that got to do with it?"

"You've been talking to your mama again, haven't you?" Randy teases. Ernestine dearly wants to be a grandmother. She's in her third year of the Civil Engineering program at the university and thrilled with the thought of holding her own grandchild in her arms on the day of her university graduation.

"Not really," Blue says, clamming up. She folds her arms and looks out the side window.

"Let's talk about Denver," Randy says.

She averts her eyes and picks small flat seeds out of her wool socks. She'd left the socks stuffed in her hiking boots since a walk up Squaw Creek in October.

He says, "What's new there?"

"Six feet of snow over last weekend."

"Look at these hills around here. Wind's blown what little there was away."

"Some people think we're headed into a long-term drought. The ski areas might close down permanently."

"In Montana? Never happen." He sips from his mug and then lodges it snugly against his crotch. "Listen, let's try to have fun. It's you and me. We know how to have a good time." His voice is persuasive, slippery, disarming.

She makes a choice – to let go for the time being. She thinks of Randy waking up in the morning, his soft long hair swirling on the pillow, his face still boyish from sleep before he's put on the mask of manhood, a kind of aloofness.

"Do you know where we're headed?" she says, pulling two maps from the backseat, from beneath their packs and the rifle.

"Check it out," he says.

They have one small photocopied map, fuzzy and difficult to read, given him by Fish and Game at the tag drawing. She matches it to the larger Forest Service map, which is confusing with all its tiny colored squares. After a few minutes, she says, "I've found it. Go past the Livingston turnoff seven miles. There's an exit that goes due north toward Clyde Park. We just stay on that road for a bit – "

"How far?"

"Quarter of an inch."

"Seriously."

"A few hundred yards, maybe. Not far. Then we turn on to a dirt road that parallels the river for a while and crosses over the ranch. Looks like bottom land, north of the river."

He follows her directions, leaving behind the snow and ice on the pass. The wind swoops up and buffets the truck. She remembers stories she's heard of pioneer women going mad from the wind, letting go of the real world, settling someplace deep inside, like gravel in a creek bed, still and safe. They pass a ranch house set up on a northern hillside, and down near the road a man in leather chaps nods to them as he opens the gate. A malamute stands sentry nearby. There are no other signs of life. The river's partially frozen over, in little riffles near the bank, and she wonders about the way it freezes, in messy chunks, and she tries to imagine the river flowing and then reaching the freezing point, caught in motion, like someone seized in a snapshot with her eyes blinking. Or someone trapped by unexpected events and then staying that way, sculpted and still, never-changing, like Lot's wife, a pillar of salt for looking back. She tries to remember the story but can't. All she can dredge up from summer Bible camp when she was five is the memory of the sticky-sweet taste of grape Kool-Aid mixed with powered sugar icing spread on graham crackers.

"You'd think this place'd be crawling with game," Randy says. "Keep your eyes peeled."

"I am."

There's ragged rimrock to the north, patched with orange and green lichen. To the south, the bottom land is stubbled and brown, falling away into the river.

"Look," she says, pointing to a gully edged in scrubby juniper. "That looks like the kind of place deer would hang out."

"You're right. Let's go a little farther. If nothing looks better we'll come back."

They drive a mile or so more until they arrive at the remains of a burned homestead, a toppling fieldstone chimney, surrounded by the abandoned everyday things of another era, a rusted wood cookstove, an iron bed frame, dented sections of stovepipe, the wooden handle of a food mill. Randy stops in the middle of the road.

"Someone lived here," he says.

"Wonder what happened to them?" Blue says, and secretly she wonders if there'd been a woman in the house and if she'd been glad to go.

"Hard to tell. They put in a lot of work for nothing."

He does a U-turn at a wide spot in the road and they return to the gully. When Blue gets out of the truck the wind bullies her around. She snaps the grippers on her vest and slips into a mesh orange hunting shirt.

"How far do you think we'll go?" she says.

"Hard to tell," Randy says, the heel of his hand on the rifle bolt's lock.

"I'll take my pack."

"Good plan," he says absently.

They cross the road and then the barbed wire fence. At the head of the gully, about five hundred feet from the truck,

Randy says, "You head down there and I'll walk around the rim. Walk slow. Don't be too quiet. You want to scare one up."

The desperate January wind blows hard and can't be ignored. Blue picks her way down the slope and the gully turns into a narrow canyon, much longer and deeper than she had imagined from the road. Her pack feels heavy, the hard edge of the Thermos cutting in her shoulder blade. Once she slips on an icy rock. She waves to him just as he disappears from her sight and then wonders if her pace is okay – too slow or too fast. She worries about being in his line of fire.

There's metamorphosed snow in the gully, crusty and gray. She creeps under some deadfall timber and remembers stealthy games she and her sister used to play as children, with bows and arrows made from green sticks and string. She's in the gully bottom when she sees the doe.

Her eyes are round, opaque brown, dumb and wise. She's lying in the snow, her head alert, staring right at Blue. Blue's heart beats faster and she stands stock-still, fifteen feet away, thinking, "You better get up and run or you're done for." For a brief moment she considers ignoring the doe, doing a little detour around her, and saying nothing to Randy. She backs up the hill, keeping an eye on the deer, until Randy happens into her line of vision again. She waves and he waves back in a friendly way. More insistent, she signals him with crossed arms above her head until he moves in her direction. She stumbles up the last hill separating them, over scab rock and through some tangled low-lying brush. Her felt-pac boots are one size too large and they blunder around on her feet uncomfortably.

"There's one down there," she says.

"Where?"

"At the bottom. She didn't move."

"Go back down and throw a few rocks at her."

Blue goes back into the gully, stooping for rocks and slipping them into her vest pocket. Under her wool cap her hair is wet from sweat, her scalp and forehead itchy. She wants to shed some layers, dispel the wind, sit down and relax, but time seems crucial, urgent. She tosses the rocks at the deer, whispering, "Go on. Let's get it over with."

The doe doesn't move; Blue realizes something's wrong with her. No wild animal would be like that. She trudges up the hill again. The wind is driving her crazy; it's like listening to fusion jazz.

"I think she must be sick or something," she says.

"Must be," Randy says. "Or she'd bolt." He holds the rifle parallel to his body, barrel up, in close to the shoulder, his finger on the trigger. The rifle's grip cap is made of swirling bird's-eye maple and Blue feels mesmerized by its beauty – it's like an agate, an unexpected find at the beach. "I'll go see," he says.

Blue waits at the rim while he goes down, out of sight. In three minutes he's back.

"There's no blood," he says. "But she didn't move."

"Should we kill her?"

"I don't know."

"We don't want to eat her if she's sick."

"No," Randy says. "On the other hand, you don't want to leave her here for some coyote."

"Could we tell if something's wrong? When you gut her?"

"Maybe." He slings the rifle over his shoulder by its leather strap. "Let's walk and think about it."

This time they stay together, plodding through the snow along the rim. The sky is drab, the land empty, as far as Blue can see. Without saying why, at the head of a side canyon, they separate, Randy heading downhill and Blue keeping to the rim. She thinks of the chocolate bar in her pack and what a lot of trouble it would be to dig it out. She's disappointed they found the doe so soon. It feels like picking asparagus from the garden rather than hunting. She wonders if they'll walk as far as the river, and then, startled, near a broad juniper, she spots blood, enough to fill a quarter-cup measure, pale on old snow. She looks over the area and there's more, a few drops, trailing away east in the same direction from which they'd come. Randy's far away. She winds around the rim in his direction until the blood peters out. She crosses deep and crusty snow, breaking through up to her knees with each step. Randy moves in a graceful diagonal up the steep slope to meet her.

"I found blood."

"Where?"

"Up there." She points to the juniper.

"Let's go take a look."

They cross the heavy snow again and go directly to the bloody trail, wordless in the wind.

Randy crouches and sweeps the bloody snow with his fingers, as though picking up crumbs. "Hard to tell how old it is," he says.

"It's from her, I'll bet."

"Could be. Let's follow it."

The blood guides them toward the gully.

"Not much of a hunt," Randy says.

"Are you going to?"

"She's injured. I feel sorry for her."

"What if she's infected?"

"If the meat looks bad we'll leave her here."

"Can we get in trouble for that?"

"If anyone knew. Maybe."

"Maybe it won't be."

"I'm going down."

"I'll wait here." Blue doesn't want to see the death throes, the last hopeless gasping. She's seen it and seen it and she never gets used to it. The blunt burst of the knife against the flesh of the throat returns in her imagination for days after a hunt.

Randy descends the slope and abruptly takes his stance, legs wide, rifle to his shoulder. He fires and scrambles further down into the gully bottom, out of sight again. Blue inches down, giving the doe time to die. It's windless down in the gully, the snow packed down and stained with urine. The doe's hind legs jerk and Randy stands over her, at close range, and fires again.

"She tried to run this time," he says.

"No kidding."

"It's her leg. One of her hind legs's been shot away at the joint. Look at this."

Blue moves in closer, her hands in her vest pockets, and examines the leg with her eyes only. The lower portion of one hind leg dangles by a few ligaments, a dirty olive green, infected.

"Coyotes would've attacked her," Randy says. "Poor thing. Wonder how long she's been here." He thrusts the butt end of his rifle in the snow, takes off his mesh hunting vest and his wool shirt, and rolls up his sleeves. The doe's head has exploded from the last shot, her prickly tongue lolling from her mouth, one side of her face blown away. The spray of blood under her head is fan-shaped. Blue feels oddly detached, as though she'd spilled a kettle of hot jam on the kitchen floor. It's that kind of major mess. She doesn't want to get bloody, but she does what she can, moves the packs, braces the rear legs apart, while Randy does all the dirty work, down on his knees, his arms inside the doe up to his elbows. Her entrails steam on the snow. Three canny ravens sail above them, croaking and flapping their wings.

Blue looks at the droppings littering the ground and says, "She's been here a while."

"I think she's okay," Randy says, leaning into the concave interior of the rib cage and sniffing.

"No wind down here."

"That's a relief."

He has several skeins of rope and clothesline, which he ties around the doe's neck and forelegs. His knots are precise, tight.

"Bombproof," he says, attaching the ropes by carabiners to wide sky-blue straps of nylon webbing; they wear the webbing like bandoleers.

"Let's come back for the packs," she says.

"And the rifle."

"I'm ready."

"Now we'll have to pull together," he says. "To share the load."

So long as she doesn't look in the doe's eyes, the deer is just meat to Blue. They struggle through the brush, one step at a time, hauling the carcass over deadfall and rocks. Stew and steaks, she thinks, her breathing growing labored.

Before starting up the final slope, they stop and rest. Cheat grass protrudes through the snow at oblique angles, like scarecrow stuffing. Randy grins and teases, "Mush, you husky."

Halfway up they stop again. "You're a good soldier, Blue," he says. "Buy you a kamikazi when we get to Livingston."

She says, "Now we're making something happen." And she wonders if this is what the fifth stage of love feels like and if it could somehow lead to Denver.

Slinkers

"THAT HOUSE has gone to rack and ruin since they moved in," my father said. Then he picked up the *Wall Street Journal* and shook it dismissingly. Aunt Margie freshened his coffee. She had an unobtrusive way of moving around him, serving him, without him ever noticing her. At ten, I was only beginning to observe the behavior of grown-ups with a clinical eye.

Our house was on a small rise and we could see into the Slinkers' back porch from our breakfast nook. Someone had busted their lattice work wall that the yellow roses climbed in July. The workbench on the porch was littered with gobs of drying raw wool. Lily's Avon bottle collection snaked along the railing. A tower of nesting clay pots teetered on the steps. Next to the steps there was an old copper washtub they wanted to use to hold firewood in the winter. And two cars rested on cement blocks – a red and white Corvette and a pale blue Malibu. There were bikes and more bikes, at least two for each Slinker, and a dented Mad River canoe. We lived in a subdivision east of Bozeman, within view of Interstate 90. From our redwood deck we could see the Spanish Peaks. The Slinkers' house had been the original farmhouse when the land had been a family farm, before the developer came along. With its gingerbread trim, painted black, their house stood out like a beaded vintage dress among a row of sleek Calvin Kleins.

"Looks lived-in to me," I said.

"*Lived-in?*" Aunt Margie said, her lips set in a grim rectangle. "Becca, where did you pick up that expression?" She said it as though I'd caught a contagious disease.

I shrugged.

I'd learned that expression from Joanne Slinker. There were five of them: the mother, Joanne; the father, Ned; and the children, Jennifer, Lily, and Moonlight, whose given name was Karen. They'd arrived in Bozeman the weekend after Easter, during a bellywomper snowstorm. This was in 1973. Joanne was a weaver and planned to study fine arts at the university and Ned had signed a contract to teach social studies at the high school. They'd come from Arizona and they all had tans; I fell in love with them immediately.

My mother died of leukemia when I was four years old. I do remember certain things. At that time in my life, we lived in town in a little shingled house with an arched entryway and brown squirrels in the backyard trees; sometimes we'd call the squirrels by tapping a wooden clothespin on the sidewalk. I remember sitting on the basement steps while she ran the laundry through the wringer, flattening the corduroy, the oxford-cloth shirts into stiff bundles that made me think of a taffy factory. Sunlight pearled in the empty pitted blue canning jars on the shelf behind her. She'd sing as she worked and the sound of my mother's singing was like a feather bed or hot cocoa crowned with marshmallows, a comfort so palpable that when she sang, nothing else existed for me. *Oh I had someone else before I had you and I'll have someone after you're gone. Streetcars and sweethearts never worry me, there will be another one along.* And I remember her dressing table, kidney-shaped, with a homemade cotton skirt printed with cabbage roses. The skirt was pleated and tacked to the dressing table with upholstery tacks; the upholstery tacks had lions' heads on them. Her dresser was thick with bottles of nail polish and lipsticks: Kiss Me Pink and Deep Deep Red. Once she painted my lips and said, "You're like Snow White," but I didn't know who Snow White was for sure. I confused her with Cinderella. I remember the way her hair fell over her forehead, in a straight blond swath, when she knelt down to tie my shoes. That's all I remember, though I try sometimes to remember more.

Aunt Margie, my father's sister, had been divorced from Uncle Chick, for reasons I never understood. She came to live with us while my mother was dying, and then she just stayed on. My father is a thin man with a concave chest, fine hair the color of wet newspapers, and a quiet dictatorial manner. This is how he was when I was ten and I'd still describe him that way today. He works for Farmer's Insurance. His pleasures seem to be keeping his accounts, and smoking an occasional cigar on the deck with Uncle Chick, who still comes around. Aunt Margie doesn't allow cigar smoking in the house. After my mother died, Aunt Margie soon organized our house on the principle of hospital corners. Every drawer had its purpose, every piece of linen its peculiar fold. She had a special brush for scrubbing the grooves between the ceramic tiles in the bathroom, and a special brush for cleaning the inside of the toaster. Her dusting rags were whiter and brighter than the Slinkers' tea towels. She'd once been in nurse's training; she spoke of pathogens as though we were about to be mired in them, without hope.

I never knew how deeply my father and Aunt Margie felt anything. An only child, I existed in a stupor of solitude when I wasn't at school, aching and longing for what I did not know.

When the Slinkers moved in, I recognized within days that what I had in stability – boredom I called it – they had in intensity.

Ned was political. He had posters and newspaper photos of his heroes taped in odd places throughout the house: Che Guevara inside the pot and pan cupboard, Mao over the tub, Bobby Kennedy on the lid of the stereo turntable. A news junkie, he listened to the radio news throughout the day on the university station, watched Walter Cronkite at night, and on Sundays he made a beeline for Poor Isaac's Newsstand downtown, where he bought the *Billings Gazette*, the *Seattle Post-Intelligencer*, and the *Chicago Tribune*. He'd chide Moonlight and me for going for the comics first. He always brought home donuts too and even now, years later, when I buy the Sunday paper I think of buying donuts. He adored Joanne. Joanne and Ned Slinker were my first encounter with married lust. I'd watch from the corner of my eye as he'd sneak up behind her at the sink or at her loom and nibble her neck until she turned around. And they'd kiss like they really meant it, his hand sledding down the curve of her back, her fingers in his fleecy black hair. They were better than the movies. Ned collected hats, embroidered skullcaps, tams, toques, baseball caps. He had friends all over the world and they sent him hats. Next to worldwide revolution, hats were what he wanted most. Ned was a solitary man in a world of women. We'd sometimes gang up on him for those pursuits of his we considered particularly masculine. He was a hunter. Whenever we'd feign disgust and act squeamish – a performance complete with high-pitched squeals and shivers – Ned would tweak his moustache and say, "Ladies. Let me tell you about the time we were reduced to eating snake in Grand Gulch, Utah." And the very idea would send us into spasms. He'd grown up in northern Michigan where they ate muskrat, or so he said.

Lily and Jennifer were the oldest and lived upstairs in their own studio apartment, with a private entrance and a private phone line. Lily was fourteen, Jennifer fifteen, when they first moved in. They were cyclists and kept a log of distances and speeds per hour. Jennifer swaggered when she walked and worked out with weights at the high school; one of our favorite things was to measure her muscles. She had smooth brown calves like sanded oiled wood. Lily was the beautiful one, with a snug cap of short dark red hair and eyes the green of kiwi fruit. They lived in peaceful coexistence upstairs, arguing over nothing more, that I knew of, than whether to share the Ouija board with Moonlight and me.

Moonlight and I were the same age. During the six years the Slinkers lived next door to me, she and I became blood sisters by pricking our little fingers with the tip of an X-Acto knife, started our periods in the same month, and fell in love with Dore, short for Theodore, a mad poet who was a grade ahead of us, and we decided to share him rather than fight over him. This puzzled Dore and he found another girl with more tradi-tional ideas, but not before he'd made love to Moonlight. We were fifteen. I heard the story in such detail and so many times, I began to feel as though he'd made love to me as well. She didn't like it. She said his penis was like one of Uncle Chick's slim cigars. She said he wasn't as handsome up close as he was from a distance. She said he'd closed his eyes and kept telling her she was just like the girl in one of his skin magazines. We'd thought Dore was sensitive – a poet with a soul. He had long blond hair. In my moody daydreams of him, I'd confused him with angels. In the letters we wrote after the Slinkers moved away, whenever Moonlight and I would tell one another about our romances, Dore became the symbol of Disappointment.

"He was another Dore," she'd write in her thick calligraphic script. And I'd know what that meant, another illusion stripped of its glimmer. Moonlight had a canopy bed and Ned helped us find a parachute to hang over it so that we had a haven, all slippery silver-blue nylon, and we'd lounge around under there on fat pillows like harem girls. We wanted tattoos and debated at length the merits of butterflies versus flowers. I tingled with pleasure as we became more bold in suggesting just exactly where on our bodies we should have these tattoos. Though we oohed and ahhed over Jennifer's muscles, we thought we were much more feminine than Lily and Jennifer. Ned called Moonlight and me *femmo* – the female equivalent of macho.

Joanne Slinker was the hot-wire, the source of energy in that house, a cross between Janis Joplin and Bette Midler. Her laughter always made you feel good. She was an artist and painted large splashy watercolors of androgynous women emerging from flowers. Once when she and Ned hosted a party for his fellow high-school teachers, everyone admired her paintings, and we heard her say, "Yes, when Ned first met me he just thought I was a good screw. He didn't know I could paint." Moonlight and I were in the kitchen wrapping oysters with bacon strips and we rolled our eyes. "Wonder if the principal heard that?" I said. "I hope so," Moonlight whispered. "Shake him up a little."

Joanne Slinker was good at the womanly arts. An inveterate shopper, she'd drive us downtown – all four of us – on a snowy Saturday, and we'd fervently plunder Main Street. Joanne had rules and advice about shopping, admonitions I remember to this day. Never shop for a bathing suit until you have a tan; if you have cellulite or *bludges* – that excess baggage on your thighs – never look at yourself unclothed in the dressing room mirror; if you find a pair of jeans that *really* fit, buy two pair. She believed in intuitive shopping. She'd be irresistibly drawn into a certain store, where she'd find some impossible bargain: a midnight blue leather jacket on a rack of T-shirts, slashed to half price. She'd say, "I had a feeling there was something in that store just waiting for me." She called these things her magic clothes, and she wore them when she needed special power, special attention. She thought you should never look at something you feel obsessively drawn to and then say, "That's way out of my price range." She thought, there's always layaway. There's always an early birthday present. "When you're older you can sell your blood," she'd kid. When we shopped with Joanne we were girls we never knew. We saw the daydreams of who we could be, the dream of multiple possibilities. One of Joanne's primary shopping rules was buy new makeup as often as you can; old makeup makes you feel sleazy. She'd take Moonlight and me to the cosmetic counter at the Bon and say to the clerk, "Becca's blue today. Let's do her face and cheer her up." And I'd be transformed, with exfoliants, color rubs, gels, and powders. Everything came in its own pastel flowered box and there was the promise of discovery in every purchase, like deeds to old silver mines. It's okay to run around without makeup when life's all peaches and sunshine, Joanne would say, but never go out depressed without doing your face.

If Aunt Margie had heard Joanne Slinker's language, that would have been the end of my connection with the Slinker family. I'd been reading novels from the adult shelf in the library for two years–unbeknownst to Aunt Margie. I'd seen *damn* and *hell* and *shit* in print. But Joanne said everything, shocking things. If she burnt a cookie sheet of gingersnaps, she'd say, "I sure fucked those up, didn't I?" And then she'd hoot with laughter. She believed cursing was a form of tyranny adults had over children. *Do as I say and not as I do.*

Joanne thought it was okay to leave the dishes until morning, that children should learn to use a washer and dryer when they're eight years old, that it was a natural human inclination to get high. She quoted some book: even little children try to change their consciousness by going around and around in playground swings. Whenever she said this, Ned would say, "That's why you go to the hairdresser, to change your consciousness." I smoked my first joint at their house, kissed my first boyfriend, nearly lost my virginity there, ate my first avocado. Joanne Slinker was the person who told me how the sperm gets to the egg; she said it like it was something to look forward to.

The stress of keeping to myself all I had learned and done at the Slinkers made me feel like a water balloon about to burst. I made a point of telling my father and Aunt Margie little tidbits of information I thought they'd approve of, to throw them off the scent. I'd say, "Mrs. Slinker made the dean's list this quarter." Or, "Mr. Slinker gives sixteen dollars a month to Save the Children." Or, "Mrs. Slinker's sister is a nun in Florida." All true statements, designed to paint a virtuous portrait of the Slinkers. Whenever I smoked grass at their house, I'd spray my hair with Estée Lauder Youth Dew to veil the smell. Whenever we had boys up to Jennifer and Lily's studio, I'd lie and say of course Mr. and Mrs. Slinker would be home. And Joanne would sometimes talk with Aunt Margie across the greening yards in spring, about Aunt Margie's lobelia, about her cat's cancer, about me. I can remember sitting hunched with Moonlight on the widow's walk, out of sight, glorying in the candy-colored, tie-dyed sunset, and listening to Joanne tell Aunt Margie how much she enjoyed me, what a fine girl I was, such ambition, I'd go far. I imagine this was the kind of talk that made Aunt Margie uncomfortable, but it was neighborly talk, and my father thought it was important to have some sort of communication with the neighbors. At least they'd call the police if they saw burglars creeping in while you were away. I began to think of our house in symbols: white bread, Mr. Clean, the double lock on the bathroom door. The most emotion I ever saw between my father and Aunt Margie was a brief bickering snarl over whether to join the group of subdivision dwellers who were petitioning the county to improve our roads. My father's chief sign of affection for her was driving her to Heeb's Supermarket every Friday night. At Slinkers' there were fights and tirades and swatting and hugging – high drama, characterized by ceremony, convoluted language, conflict, love. The Slinkers loved to talk, usually at high speed and high volume. Their communication was efficient – they often finished one another's sentences. I led a double life. Sometimes I'd stop by the lilac bushes that separated our front yards and stand there between the two worlds, breathing in the cloy of the lilacs, calming myself to move from their house to ours. Alpine glow glazed the mountains. I'd feel like the luckiest twelve-year-old in the world.

Joanne moved out twice during the six years they lived next door. The first time, the summer I was twelve, she moved into a boxy little pre–World War II house on campus, with a woman she thought she'd fallen in love with, another art student. Her name was Shandell Walks-on-Water; she was from a reservation up on the Hi-Line. I saw them together only once before Aunt Margie got wind of the whole scandal at church and forbade me to ride my bike into town to see them. That one time – a sunny day in July, the mountain air finespun – Moonlight and I ate ice cream from pie plates while Shandell and Joanne lay on their backs in chaise longues, glistening with coconut oil, listening to us retell the story of some horror movie we'd been to see the night before. I remember I felt privileged, inducted into a private female world. She stayed away for a month, and Ned, resigned to her doing what she felt she *had* to, spent the month fishing at Ferry Lake.

The second time she moved out, Moonlight and I were fifteen, old enough to figure out how to take full advantage of the situation. Joanne had met a ski instructor at Bridger – a man who didn't talk much, as far as Moonlight and I could tell, and we weren't sure what she saw in him. Moonlight had a theory that it was the adventurer in him Joanne liked. He'd skied on four continents. He wore a silver chain on his wrist he claimed some Gypsies in Spain had given him.

We were all taking skiing lessons that winter, except for Ned, who was embroiled in teachers' union politics. He said he wouldn't have time for skiing until after the revolution. He was at a conference in Helena the first evening Joanne stayed with her ski instructor.

That Sunday night, Moonlight and I rode the ski bus home, as far as McDonald's, and then Lily and her boyfriend picked us up in his station wagon. We'd met some boys on the slopes – they were older than we were, seniors at a private school in Colorado, still on Christmas break, visiting their Bozeman cousins. They were crazy skiers, reckless, and at that time in our lives Moonlight and I were attracted to what we called bad boys. We'd given them Slinkers' address and invited them over. I can still remember standing outside the ski bus at the bottom of the mountain, in the grip of the wind, the darkening sky as blue as my lapis lazuli earrings, my fingers stiff as I wrote out directions on the back of a cash register receipt. The one I liked was Rob. He was tall and hovered over me. There was something raw and new in the pull I felt toward him. Before we parted he kissed me roughly and left my face wet and chapped, and when I got on the bus and saw Moonlight, I grinned an idiot grin.

At the Slinkers' we conferred. Joanne had said she'd be home by the time Ned was home. Ned would be home by ten. We had four hours. Jennifer was at the library – she was a clerk in circulation. Lily and her boyfriend – he'd been president of the Honor Society the year before – went upstairs, giggling at us. "Be good, girls," Lily said, "at whatever you do."

I went home to clean up. The uncertainty of our plans, my fragile state of erotic chaos, made me stealthy. I ever so quietly propped my skis against the garage door. My father was on a late elk hunt up near Yellowstone. I imagined Aunt Margie was watching television. I opened the back door silently and moved soundlessly into the hall. The clock chimed the half hour. Aunt Margie had been cooking with garlic. A dim light from the kitchen looked yellow on the waxy hall tiles. It was possible to get to my room without passing any door but the kitchen. I was in my sneakers. I passed the kitchen and kept on walking, and my brain did not register at first what I'd seen. In my room, I reviewed. Aunt Margie and Uncle Chick had been standing at the sink, kissing. She'd looked soft and limp, her blouse pulled out of her slacks. Uncle Chick wore a maroon velour pullover and his gray beard was neatly trimmed. His big belly had pressed against her insistently. Her hair had been mussed. I kept thinking, *but they're divorced*. I turned on the radio so they would know I was there.

After my shower, when I was dressed and ready to go, I leaned against the door frame between the living room and the dining room and said, "Hi. How's everything?" Tucked in my jeans pocket were two rubbers Moonlight I had bought at a drugstore in Billings when we went to a Heart concert.

They were watching a black-and-white movie, a TV tray of beer and cashews between them.

"Fine as wine," Uncle Chick said, without looking my way.

"Did you have a good ski lesson, Becca?" Aunt Margie said. She twisted around sprightly in her chair. I tried to remember how old they were.

I said, "I fell down a few times."

"There's leftovers in the oven," Aunt Margie said.

"I want to spend the night at Slinkers'."

"It's Sunday," she said, turning back to the movie.

"We have homework," I said. "We're drilling each other on the periodic table."

"All right, all right," she said. "I suppose you'd wear me down if I kept saying no. Try to get to bed at a decent hour."

And I was gone, feeling crafty, that exhilaration you're pumped full of when you think you're free, free at last. The moon was out as I crossed from our yard to theirs, the old snow frozen in a smooth hard slab that reminded me of suet we put out for the chickadees. My thighs ached from skiing.

Moonlight and I were nearly hysterical with anticipation. We weren't sure they'd come. She sat on the toilet seat while I curled my eyelashes and rolled on inky black mascara. We felt we could do whatever we wanted with them, because they were from Colorado. We wouldn't have to live with the consequences. I showed her the rubbers. When I look back on those times, it is hard for me to imagine that we were the same girls who argued reasonably on the debating team, who ran for student council, who wrote heartfelt political letters to the editor of the school paper. It was as though our minds simply stopped functioning when we felt the rowdy urge to be bad girls, to break every rule ever made.

The doorbell rang and Moonlight went to answer it. I put some music on the stereo. Rob and his friend Jim stepped into the house, chanting, "I see London, I see France, I see some-one's underpants." They'd been drinking. Moonlight and I looked – perplexed – at one another and laughed. They were dressed in tweed overcoats and brought the cold in with them, and something else, a presence that separated Moonlight and me, diluted our connection. Before they'd arrived, we'd been like lovers, or as I imagine lovers could be, in my more idealistic moments, close enough to be real. When they arrived we picked up a dialogue of pretense like some skit we were auditioning for. I could see we were doing this, but that knowledge was below the surface, the nagging thought that we were being phony like an evanescent fish under a frozen lake.

At first we sat around the kitchen table and talked about our schools. Theirs was all boys. They said for fun they went out to Boulder and tried to get in the bars and drank drinks with names like Slippery Nipple. They skied at Mary Jane on the weekends. They'd both been accepted at three universities. Rob wanted to be an officer in the Air Force.

Moonlight told them she wanted to study cultural anthropology. "Oh, yeah?" Jim said. "My mother's into that. Lots of girls are."

The light in the kitchen had a dimmer switch and in due time I dimmed it, on my way to the fridge for a beer. Someone suggested we dance. Later, when I told Lily about dimming the light, she said, "The rest is history." But the whole experience didn't turn out at all the way I'd expected or hoped.

Rob and I soon maneuvered ourselves privacy, in the greenhouse that jutted out from the kitchen to catch the southern sun. Tomatoes and basil grew in black plastic tubs there. The white pebbles rolled under our feet, and we giggled and leaned against one another. I had on a rayon blouse that I thought felt like nightgown material. When he pulled me by the waist, his hand large and adamant, I thought right then that I'd do anything he wanted to do. There were purple grow lights in the greenhouse and an old dusty red car seat. We sat down on the car seat and started kissing. The place smelled like herbs and dirt. He moved along pretty fast, into my blouse. At first it felt good, pushing my breasts into his hands, then he leaned down and started sucking one of my nipples. That hurt. I tried to urge him back to my face, but he wasn't interested. I looked down at his hair and his scalp was flaky; something about that revolted me.

"Oh my God," I said.

"What's wrong?" he said, not bothering to take his mouth completely away from me. His finger flicked the copper-colored zipper tab on my jeans.

"I just started my period," I said.

His shoulders slumped. "Oh baby."

"I know. It's awful, isn't it? I'll have to go to the bathroom. Be right back."

I extricated myself from his grasp and half-hopped, half-hobbled out of the greenhouse, out of the Slinkers', across the yard to my house. Yellow light from our kitchen leached into the snow. I stood there without my jacket, buttoning my blouse, letting the cold freeze his spit on my breast. I wanted the comfort of my own room, with its dull corduroy bed-spread, the horse pictures on the wall. My jeans were so tight I could feel the seams chafing the insides of my legs.

I sneaked in my bedroom window. I tiptoed to the bath-room and scrubbed my face and chest with Dial soap. I brushed my teeth for about five minutes. Then I brought the phone into my bedroom from the hallway, and called Lily and told her I'd left and that she might want to check on Moonlight. Then I put on a flannel nightgown and climbed into my bed.

I left my door open. I lay there wide awake for a long time, so relieved, just repeating to myself, *he wasn't the right one to be the first one.* After a little while, I turned on the radio very low and listened to the kind of music they play on a Sunday night, some sad country, and I listened to the house sounds too, and thought how fine they were, the clock chiming every half hour, the water filter purring in the aquarium in the living room, the rustle of my own blankets. I thought about my mother and wondered if she could see everything I did. I didn't think so. I'd stopped believing in heaven when I was thirteen. I wondered if she had lived if she'd have been the kind of mother who'd have told me about how the sperm gets to the egg. Then, as I lay there, loving my aloneness, Uncle Chick walked by my door on the way to the bathroom. He had on big white boxer shorts that seemed to incandesce in the dark like the face of an alarm clock. And I thought about how everyone has a secret life of some sort, a private array of lusts and sins and longings and dreams, even Ned at his conference and my father on his elk hunt. Right before I drifted away into sleep, I had this picture in my mind of human beings all over the world, squirming with longing, their arms open to one another, waiting to be touched.

Labrador

FINALLY, we were moving.

My mother stood in the dirt section of the yard, beside the green pump, holding the rooster Pete in her arms the way you might a kitten. His feet clawed against air. A neighbor woman was there and my mother was readying herself to transfer Pete to her, knowing full well that, with this woman, there was no sentimentality about roosters, and, tough as he was, he'd be in a pot on the stove before nightfall. Pete was the last chicken left of a flock that'd been slaughtered early one morning by an unknown dog in a messy, cruel way. I don't think my mother ever completely recovered from the shock of finding the torn-up chickens under the pear tree. I didn't understand this then, when I was fifteen, but now I do. It was a violation, like having your face slapped or your pocket picked, and a lifetime of just such seemingly small violations can leave you worn out and sad, nearly depleted of dreams.

Though she was putting on a happy face for the move. We all were. My father had taken a job in the state of Maryland, at the telephone company in Rising Sun. To get there, we would have to cross the states of Ohio, West Virginia, Pennsylvania, all of it unexplored territory. I'd never been further from home than Indianapolis. I longed to be a traveler and had a book I planned to read on the way, a dog-eared paperback about the Amazon Basin.

"Good luck and all that," the neighbor woman said. My mother handed her the rooster. They'd known each other nine years. I don't think they knew what to say or that it was possible for them to imagine each other's absence.

My mother sidled toward the Rambler, waving over her shoulder. She was wearing new madras Bermuda shorts and a sleeveless white blouse. "Don't forget to write," she said. I thought they would write to one another, but I don't believe they ever did. Like a schoolgirl she added, "Don't do anything I wouldn't do."

We children – all seven of us – and two dogs, one cat, and my father, had been waiting impatiently in the cars. Bingo, the Saint Bernard, didn't like to travel. We'd gotten tranquilizers from the vet and he lay passive as a rug in the back of the blue-and-white Ford station wagon. The plan, elaborated on, refined in detail over many evenings, was this: Mother would drive the Rambler with me, the oldest, and the two youngest, Maureen and Colleen. My father would take the four boys – David, Kevin, Stephen, and Joe – and the animals. Big Bopper, the long-haired black cat; Bingo; and Rummy, an old female beagle who'd had more litters of pups than I could remember. We had headlight signals and signs to communicate between the two cars. We'd picked a place on the map to stop for the night: Zanesville, Ohio. There was much concern and talk about losing one another on the interstate highway. But my father assured us that would not happen and I believed him.

We drove away and I don't think anyone looked back, though perhaps my mother did and I didn't want to notice. I didn't understand then about the pain of moving or what we might be relinquishing to do so. Now I know that my mother had for years fanned a spark – a dream – about that place in the country, and the dream had to do with chickens and pear trees and blackberries and children roaming the woods. Not an unusual dream, naive and touching when I think of it now. Perhaps my father shared that dream with her, though of that I'm less certain. That ordinary frame farmhouse and seven acres had been given to my parents by my mother's father, who lay dying of emphysema in the front bedroom of his house on South Seventh Street in Terre Haute. My mother loved him dearly, but somehow she was able to leave him, able to give up the predictability of our life in Indiana – for she and my father had both been born there, on the south side of Terre Haute, just blocks from one another – in exchange for the risk of a new turn in the road, one none of us had expected. We were going to get on in the world without grandparents and aunts and uncles. Since then, of course, I've wrenched my love away from many places and people, and my heart goes out to my mother for what she must have experienced. I wish I could tell her that now. When parents die young, you become old before your time, living in the past with them, in memory. You think they'll never know how much like them you've become, but it's possible they did know. It's possible she knew what I would become before I did, and I console myself with that.

We followed our plan and arrived three days later at the house my father had rented for us, a big Victorian in the country, with a fireplace, a creek across the property, an empty lot for softball next to a cornfield, a screened-in back porch on the second floor, and bedrooms enough for me to have my own room. We never knew how old and drafty the house was until winter. My mother would put on an extra sweater and curse the house then, because, by that time, the reason we'd moved had unraveled like cheap goods.

This move took place in the summer of 1963. Before that I

hadn't thought of my parents as people who had dreams that might be dashed. I knew that there were difficulties between them and that those difficulties had to do with money and drinking and gambling. There was a shadow of another problem, possibly having to do with other women in my father's life. But that was never mentioned outright in the arguments I overheard. My thinking on that comes from a memory of when I was four years old: my father arriving home late at night in a yellow taxi, my mother meeting him on the street, screaming and striking out at him. She and I had been watching a late movie on television. On the porch, in my pajamas, I could see my breath. My mother's loafers kicked up the ankle-deep sycamore leaves on the sidewalk, a cutting sound. A caved-in pumpkin rotted on the porch next to the white milk box. Now that I have been married twice, and twice divorced, I know the sound of jealous screaming. There's a powerlessness to it, like a wounded animal that cares only for its own hurt. That's how my mother was screaming that night. Still, I never heard her mention it afterwards. The root of the trouble seemed to be that my father worked away from home. In order to be at home with us, my father had to take jobs that were beneath him. At the meat-packing plant or the glass factory, work like that. He had taken those jobs for a year, here and there. Otherwise, he'd worked away from home; he was a telecommunications wizard, a crackerjack. Everyone said so and I imagine that is true, since my brothers have turned out the same. That is, they work as electronics engineers and one of them, the youngest, before the age of thirty, has risen to a position of prominence in one of those long-distance companies that make your phone bill so complicated. My father discovered his genius in the Philippines during World War II. The Army taught him what he knew. When he returned home to Terre Haute and married my mother, who'd also been in the war, telecommunications was still all he knew and loved and he took what opportunity came his way, in spite of babies being born right and left. He went to work on the DEW line in Labrador, and after that, on installations in New York and Pennsylvania and Michigan. My mother was always pregnant and my father was always gone. She used to say he came home just often enough to make a new baby. He used to say my sister Colleen looked suspiciously like the milkman; that was one of his standard jokes. He traveled, leaving in the tang of aftershave, with leather suitcases, and when he came home for visits, we'd meet him at the train station across from the Wabash Cigar Store, and he'd bring home green boxes of pastry and Chicago newspapers. And there was always that trouble between them, and the trouble would flare up at night when he was home for a visit. I would lie awake in my bedroom and wait for it in dread. That dread had become something that was always with me, that I was ashamed of, as much a part of me as a humiliating middle name might have been, or a birthmark I'd want to hide. It had been made clear to me, mostly through eavesdropping, that in making this move my father was making a promise to change his ways. He would come home for supper every night—that's how my mother phrased it. They envisioned family life in this new place, and, listening to them, I believed it was possible.

THAT SUMMER, I wanted only to read and be kissed. I did my chores without being asked, then squirreled away in cool places, going back and forth between what even then I knew were junk books—romances, nurse stories—and literature. Willa Cather. Victor Hugo. I turned sixteen in August and had been casting about for someone to kiss. My brothers had made quick friends, softball buddies, but they seemed too young, sweaty, pimply, their voices still high. Not that I was any dream girl. There was a scholarly sluggishness about me, I knew. I wore glasses. And my clothes seemed to fit me oddly, clumsily. But in ninth grade, I'd been told I had bedroom eyes by a Latin teacher who drove an Austin Healey and couldn't've been over twenty-three. I knew it was out of the ordinary to be told this by a teacher and that there were probably rules he was breaking to do so. I hoarded the remark, turning it over and over in the dark of night, knowing there was shame in having been told that, but also pride. In spite of everything that had been drilled into me – and insinuated – about the difference between good girls and bad girls, my body was ready, keen as a trained falcon. I knew from reading that erotic pleasure was a force to be reckoned with, perhaps the most powerful force. I thought of it as sudden, transformational, a little like severe, unexpected weather.

Up a long and winding hill, past a dairy farm with violet salt blocks in the pasture, lived another large family, the Karskis. They were Catholic too, and like us, their father had worked away most of their lives. He was in the Navy. They were older than we were, with girls still at home who'd graduated or quit school. Their youngest was ten. Their mother was a jolly-faced portly woman who took for granted that some of the time we would break rules or yearn to be wild. She'd take us to movies at the naval base and keep watch from afar in the outdoor amphitheater as we flirted with the swabbies. They'd let us wear their glowing white caps, but it never went any further than that with me, even though I thought I wanted it to. Charleen, the oldest Karski, must've been taking it further somewhere else, because she was married early that fall to a sailor about to ship out for the Mediterranean. It was common knowledge she was pregnant, though we didn't call it that, of course; we only said she'd gotten herself in trouble.

There was to be a party after the ceremony, on a school night, at the Karskis. I thought I would get my kiss at that party, I was determined. My mother would be in attendance for a little while, but she would go home early, to get the little ones ready for bed. Mrs. Karski had already interceded for me and gotten my mother's permission for me to stay on. She'd promised to bring me home herself. I had the idea no one else from the high school would be there. The guests would all be sailors and Charleen's friends who'd graduated the year before. It seemed like the safest place, in terms of reputation, to get a kiss. I gave much thought to locations: behind the latticework on the side porch or in the back stairwell, what had once been the ser- vants' staircase, when the house had been a finer house.

I itched for my mother to leave. She had two pieces of wed- ding cake and had asked Mrs. Karski for an extra sugar rose. This mortified me, though I'd thought of asking for an extra sugar rose myself. She wanted to see the newlyweds – every- one called them that – open their presents.

Charleen and Bobby were in the kitchen and it was clear that's where the real party was, with loud music playing – the Supremes – and drinking. They'd made something called artil- lery punch. I'd passed in and out of the kitchen a couple of times, afraid to join them, longing to. Sailors were lounging in a row against the counter and seeing them there, in that small room, with their starchy summer uniforms tight across their hips, I realized they were men, all grown up in a way I certainly was not. Charleen's girlfriends were there, too, smoking Swisher Sweets, whispering in the ears of the sailors. The room felt freighted with sexual tension. Weddings are like that some- times; I know that now, but then I thought all that desire was knotted in me and emanated from me.

My mother and Mrs. Karski and a few children and the old women neighbors sat in the living room drinking tea, or sherry in little blue glasses that still had oval POLAND stickers on the bottoms. They passed the time with talk of squash reaped and winter's prospects. I sat falsely dutiful near my mother on a hassock.

"It's dark," I said once, thinking to remind her of her own departure.

"Yes, the nights are coming on sooner now," she said.

"I wonder if Dad's home yet?"

"Well, I wouldn't worry," she said. "David's there. He's nearly fourteen now. You shouldn't have to do it all." She meant all the baby-sitting. She swept my bangs to one side of my forehead in what I knew was an affectionate gesture, but I hated it. I jerked away, more abruptly than I'd intended.

She sniffed and shrugged, to cover her hurt feelings. She hadn't dressed for the party and I was ashamed to see her there in bobby socks and blue jeans, with a kids' barrette in her hair. I felt bad about hurting her feelings and being ashamed, but they seemed like responses I couldn't resist or control. These were venial sins I often confessed of a Saturday so that I could take communion on Sunday.

"No rest for the wicked," she said, to no one in particular. She got up to go and I felt it was a fragile moment, that she might change her mind.

"I'll walk out with you," I said.

At her car, she said, "Don't drink yet, Kate."

"What makes you think I will?"

"Don't swell up like a toad now," she said. "I'm telling you this for your own good."

She got in then and I turned and went back to the house before a real argument happened, one that might make her take me home. I watched from just inside the front door until her taillights disappeared.

The kitchen was dim and blue with smoke. There was dancing and loud laughter. Someone grabbed me as soon as I
walked in the door.

"Here's a gal might be able to cowboy jitterbug," he said,
shoving me into the middle of the kitchen. He was short and
drunk.

It was a kind of dancing I'd never done before, where you
hold hands and the man leads you, swirls you. It would've
been hard enough to do sober, but he tripped on his own
black shoes.

Someone shouted, "Hank is from Wyoming, honey. You
got to have a cowboy hat to learn to dance like that."

I pulled away and went over to Charleen, as though I had an
important message for her. "He's weird," I whispered. I stared
at a holy card of the Virgin Mary on the windowsill next to a
packet of carrot seeds.

She rolled her eyes. "I'm having morning sickness at night,"
she said. "So soon." Charleen had a big, puffy face in which I
could already see her mother. A smear of yellow cake frosting
had dried on her chin. She tipped her beer can up for the last
swallow. Then she said, "Have a drink, kid. Relax." She pushed
me toward the counter. "Robbie, give Kate a drink."

I must've looked taken aback, because Robbie put his arm
gently around my shoulder and said, "What's a nice girl like
you doin' at a party like this?" We both knew it was a joke. "I'm
Robbie. You're Kate. Let's be friends."

The tile floor was gummy with spilled beer and my flats
stuck to it. Robbie was drunk too, but he wasn't rough, and I
wanted to linger there with him, pliantly, with his arm around
my shoulder. Mrs. Karski came to the kitchen door and shook
her head and laughed.

Robbie said, "Here, honey, drink up," and he handed me a

blue aluminum tumbler, the kind I'd drunk Kool-Aid from for as long as I could remember. There was whiskey in it.

I took a sip.

"One more," he coaxed.

I took a bigger gulp, and coughed.

He squeezed my waist. "'Atta girl," he said. "You little bohemian, you." I'd never heard that word before, but it sounded like what I wanted to be. When he smiled, I saw that all of his back teeth were filled with gold. "Little more and you'll be flying high."

I'd lost my head. It tasted terrible, and the burning made me think of fireworks for some reason, those little snakes you light on the sidewalk, but the lure of experience and the desire to defy my mother pushed me on until I'd drunk about a half-tumbler of whiskey in a short time.

The party ended for me then. I had to lurch outside to the edge of the herb garden, among the chives and borage, and throw up wedding cake. I could smell the honeysuckle tangled on the latticework. Inside, Robbie was laughing, and I heard Charleen yelling at him, calling him a creep. For months afterwards my face would turn hot and red when I remembered how I squandered my desire on him. Mrs. Karski drove me home, with the windows rolled down.

My mother saw the whole story, in one knowing glance. She said, "What a sorry case you are."

I stood at the bottom of the stairs for a minute, shame-faced, my hand on the newel post for support. I knew I deserved her scorn, or even worse. I fixed my eyes on the mud I'd gotten on my stockings and shoes when I went out to throw up. The little ones were lined up on the sofa in pastel pajamas, watching television, and their innocence made me sad. I wanted to be among them again.

My mother sat in a rocking chair in her house slippers, rocking angrily, her mouth a stern straight gash. "Your father didn't come home tonight," she said.

At the time I was too drunk to understand the significance of that, and I went upstairs and tried to read Henry Esmond for English the next day, tried to push the foolish thing I'd done out of my mind.

MY FATHER didn't come home for the next three nights. At the same time, word had gotten around school about what I'd done at the party. I was left alone to eat my lunch in the cafeteria, by girls I'd been cultivating as friends. At home I was on my best behavior, helping out without being asked. For punishment, my mother was distant and spoke to me only when necessary. As the three days wore on, though, and my father still did not come home and there was no word from him, she weakened, needing me, and found small ways of letting me know I was back in her good graces. Asking about the debating team; offering me a lipstick sample given her by the Avon lady. When no one else was around, my mother would say, not directly to me, but to the space around me, "He's gone to play the ponies, no doubt. To Delaware. Or Baltimore." She knew him, she knew his patterns, she knew his weaknesses.

When he did come home, nothing was the same.

It was late on an Indian summer morning, a Sunday, after Mass. My mother had taken off her earrings and plunked them in a glass salad bowl on the buffet in the dining room. She said I could make a Chef Boyardee pizza for lunch, and that she'd fry a chicken for supper.

My father drove into the driveway, came into the house in an ordinary way, slinging his navy cardigan on the sofa, as though he'd been away for an hour running an errand. He could, once in a while, seem a happy man, energetic and up-beat. My brothers and sisters gathered around him, hungry to see him, and he let that siphon away his attention. He picked up the baby, Colleen, and held her over his head and with his lips made sounds she thought were funny against her stomach. Joe hit his leg with his little square fist, and my father knelt down and roughhoused with him for a few minutes, trading phony punches. I went in the kitchen to start the pizza, posted myself near the door so I could hear whatever they might say. My mother sat at the round oak table in her church dress, her arms bare on the table, fiddling with an unlit cigarette.

"You kids go play now," he said. "I need to talk with your mother."

He sat down across from her, just as they'd been on so many evenings, discussing the war or some old movie or the Depression, things from their past they liked to remember. He borrowed her lighter and lit a cigarette.

He tossed some money on the table. "I won two-fifty," he said.

"How much did you lose?" she said bitterly.

"That's none of your damn business."

His tone frightened me. He was not by nature a harsh man, but he could be driven to harshness by my mother in quick spurts that surprised me.

"I'm going on the road again," he said. "It's not working out at the phone company."

"I figured as much," she said, her voice hard. And when I think of that, I wonder how much that hardness cost her. He'd moved her there with such high hopes. And now she'd be by herself, responsible for all of us, but she didn't say that. She kept that to herself.

And him, what did it cost him to give up what he'd moved

there for? We children sided with our mother, and it was many years before I could think of him and his life on the road, a life that I imagine as lacking in joy and sometimes mean. The motels; the meals in taverns; the interminable evenings.

He did spend the night. My mother did fry the chicken and he whipped the mashed potatoes and we sat down to supper together. Later they watched television, and I saw in my father a kind of leaden passivity. He wasn't forty yet and had seven children. My mother used to say the house could burn down around him and he wouldn't budge. The next morning, before we left for school, we kissed him good-bye at the bathroom door. He was bare-chested, wrapped at the waist in a towel, and half his face was lathered with shaving cream. That was the last time I saw my father for a year and a half.

My mother began changing then, but I didn't want to notice the changes.

At school I worked hard at ingratiating myself to the right people, girls who ran the yearbook, the newspaper. At my old school in Indiana, I'd been in line for responsibility and limelight. Now I had to start all over again. The gossip of my drunkenness faded as other, more serious, scandal arose, an attempted suicide in the tenth grade, vandalism of the principal's office. And then, President Kennedy was killed. We were awestruck and unified in our mourning. For months, I mooned around over the chemistry teacher, a crush shared by a boy named Seth, my first gay friend, though gay was not a word we used or had even heard of. What thrill there was in trading confidences with Seth. We felt we were destined to live beyond the boundaries, in regions of experience few but us would ever know.

I took a weekend waitress job at a Christian camp not far from home. By this time I'd stopped going to Mass and was – I told anyone who would listen – seeking a spiritual experience more satisfying. I lived at the camp on weekends, in the dorm, and listened with an open mind to the evangelical preachers, who were lean men with visionary eyes, never without their Bibles right at hand. At the same time, the staff – the waitresses and cooks and dishwashers – had their own private world at the camp, staying up in the lounge until two in the morning, with a good fire in the fireplace and the cook's little television on the hearth. We were all smart and quick of tongue and irreverence was required of us in order to belong. We were lewd in the kitchen, even while the blessing was being said in the dining room. The cook would crack eggs with one hand – plop, plop, plop – a skill I greatly admired, and he'd say, "These are my birth control glasses. Guys in black glasses never get laid." What esprit and exurberance there was in all our free talk. We thought we were daring, subversive. I still hadn't been kissed, but beyond home I had this rich life, discovering my own eccentricities, my intensity. As a daily signature, I wore a red velvet beret.

Warning signs did arise now and then to bring me back to what was happening at home. One spring evening I was reading a children's story to Maureen and Colleen. This was nearly eight months after my father had gone. We were on the front porch steps, near a rick of fragrant stacked firewood. The boys had a softball game going in the field not far from us. We could hear them egging one another on, hear the thwunk of the bat against the ball. My mother was at the dining room table – I could picture her there and hear the music she and her friend listened to: old show tunes from the fifties. She'd found a woman friend who liked to drink and the two of them sat there murmuring of an evening, smoking and drinking, either beer from a sweaty quart bottle or sometimes, if they were in the money, they'd have gin and tonics. When the tonic was gone, they'd drink the gin neat from jelly glasses. It was evening, as I said, and almost too dark to be reading, but I loved the fecund smell of spring and the sense of life going on all around us as I read aloud.

"Kitty has an owie," Colleen interrupted me.

"Oh, no," I said, just being polite to her. She was three years old.

"No, he *does*," Maureen insisted. "Momma says Big Bopper has a mikaphone in his paw." She was five and much more savvy than Colleen.

"A what?" I said.

"A secret mikaphone. Someone's listening to her secrets."

"Uh-huh," Colleen said.

"Momma's only kidding," I said.

I took them into the bathroom then and bathed them and put them to bed. I did not give any more thought to what they'd said, not for months, and I don't know if anything would have turned out differently if I had paid attention to them. I wanted to continue with my discovery of myself out in the world. Now when I remember Maureen's words, though, I see that my mother's grip was loosening months before I faced that fact. Doctors have labels for what she felt. She was suffering, at war with herself, fearful, and I didn't want to notice. Noticing was sure to make me feel powerless, unable to change what needed to be changed. If my mother could read my mind now, thinking this, she'd be fatalistic and dismissive. She'd say, Hindsight's always better than foresight. Still, I think we always have to wonder, in families, what would happen if we paid attention early on.

THE LAST WEEK of school, in June, our grandfather died.

My mother heard the news over the telephone, early one

morning, as we sat around the table eating cereal. The radio was on. Our brown lunch bags were on the table, the tops still not folded down, with milk money beside each bag. Her face turned dark red. She squeezed shut her eyes and began crying.

Stephen said, "What's wrong, Momma?"

When she hung up the receiver, she picked up her cigarettes and went in the kitchen. We all looked at one another uneasily, questioningly. She moaned, a cry that hurt my heart to listen to. She banged on the cupboard door above the counter. Then she came back to us and we were stunned and openmouthed around the table.

"Your grandpa's dead now," she said, still crying. Her face puckered with sorrow and shock.

Maureen went over to her and took her hand. None of the rest of us knew what to do; we were old enough to be embarrassed by death. We knew it was a solemn moment, but, ignorant of the right thing to do, we only wanted to get away.

"Bus's coming," Joe called from the front room window. He'd slipped away from the table as soon as he saw her tears.

That was our cue and my brothers and I left her there alone with the two little girls. She had no one with whom to share that grief, and I imagine she felt lonely then, more lonely than she ever had, since marriage, if it serves us at all, serves us during those times of loss.

In the late afternoon, at the end of study hall, my name was called out over the loudspeaker. My mother met me near the principal's office, next to the trophy case. The floor was waxed brightly all around her, and amid that shine and order, she looked all the more downcast, beyond comfort. She hadn't combed her hair and she wore a pair of muddy irrigators. They were David's. He worked at the dairy farm on Saturdays. It had been raining all morning and I thought she must have been out walking in the rain. Her face seemed swollen from crying.

"Kate, I want you to go to Grandpa's funeral," she said.

I was surprised and I'm certain my face revealed that.

"You're going on an airplane. You've never been on an airplane before."

"Who's paying for it?" I said. I couldn't imagine we had money for airplanes.

"Never you mind," she said. "Money's been set aside."

"It's the last week of school."

"The principal says it's okay."

While we were talking, she pushed me out the double glass doors. I think she felt uneasy at school; she rarely went there.

In the car I said, "Why don't *you* go?"

She started crying and put her arms around the steering wheel. "I just can't," she said, through her tears. Then she straightened up and wiped her eyes on her flannel sleeve. She rummaged in her tooled leather purse for a handkerchief. "I'm just treading water, Kate. I can't push myself."

I believe she couldn't bear to know the truth, to see the dead, to be owned again by what she'd left behind. I don't know if she ever went back there, to Terre Haute, until she was buried there herself. Though it's possible she and my father passed through there years later, the years when I was out of touch with them, and she had gone on the road with him.

"Okay, I'll go, I guess."

"That's my big girl, Kate. Look," she said, feigning cheeriness, "I've packed a bag for you." She put the flat of her hand on a plaid suitcase in the backseat. "I'm driving you to Friendship Airport right now. You're as good as in the air."

And that is what we did. We drove to Baltimore in the light rain, with "The Buddy Dean Show" on the radio. She did not mention my grandfather or give me any messages for anyone at the funeral. Her silence roared at me. She did not speak at all, except to say, "You can stay a couple weeks if you want. Would you like that?"

I stayed there, with one of my aunts, for exactly ten days. The summer humidity had closed upon the Midwest like a vise and the funeral was held on a sweltering day. The women wore white cotton gloves and cooled themselves with paper fans printed with Bible verses. They were Protestant, the funeral service economical and plain, though my grandfather had owned his own business – the Dixie Bee Garage – and half the block it stood on. My grandmother was unapproachable; she cried in a terrifying way at odd times. Still, I liked being away from home. I'd seldom been a guest anywhere. People took care of me and that was a novelty. There were picnics and trips to the new shopping center and evenings of iced tea and layer cakes and television. I was allowed to read in bed each morning as long as I wanted. It did not seem such an unbearable thing that my grandfather had died. Being there, listening to people talk about him – exalting his virtues, forgetting his faults – it seemed only a part of life I'd never experienced before. I could almost forget home, forget mother. Almost.

The very night my mother called me home, I was kissed for the first time, on my aunt's sun porch by her stepson, Lannie. Lannie had been a greaser and a roughneck in high school, cocky with talk of cars and fistfights, and there'd been a brush or two with the law, again, having to do with cars and driving, and he had spent at least one night in jail, though he had straightened himself out by this time. He was twenty-four. He worked at an auto parts store and had a canoe and went canoeing on Sugar Creek on the weekends. He still lived at home with my aunt. His father had died of a brain tumor, leaving my aunt a widow for the second time.

This particular evening, she had gone to my grandmother's house. Strawberries were coming in and my aunt was afraid my grandmother, sick with grief, would let them go to waste. Lannie and I were in the house alone. The temperature had been in the nineties and the house seemed to pulse with the heat. I'd been reading in my room, the front bedroom, with the window fan turned on high. I had my hair done up in sponge rollers. When I went to the kitchen for a drink of ice water, I heard music from the sun porch and went out there to investigate.

The wooden venetian blind slats were shut against the evening sun. Lannie sprawled in an easy chair of red cracked leather, eyes closed, with his ear next to the big radio, the Roosevelt radio my aunt always called it, since she associated that radio with listening to Roosevelt during the war. The walls were knotty pine, the light a dim gold in the room.

I had never heard music like that before and I felt irresistibly drawn to it. Now I know it's called delta blues. Lightnin' Hopkins. Bessie Smith. But that was my first exposure to the blues, to the physical clutch of it, that sensual gift.

Lannie squinted, and when he saw me there, enthralled, he mutely patted the chair arm, motioning me to sit down. I went to sit beside him on the arm of the chair, though there were other places to sit on the sun porch. It seemed most natural – and dangerous – to be perched there beside him. He had on the cleanest blue jeans and a white shirt, the sleeves rolled up on his forearms. By that time, the forearms of men had begun to intrigue me; I liked the sunny pattern of blond hair growing on his arm near the wrist, the way the veins intruded softly on the underside. He wore sandals and his feet were tanned. My aunt had always said he'd be a heartbreaker when he grew up, be able to wrap women around his little finger. He had dark, coppery curls and his eyelashes were sunbleached on the tips.

In one hand he held a harmonica, gently kept time with it against his thigh. The other hand, within minutes, he had placed against the small of my back and he left it there, warm and firm, while we listened to the music.

The program ended at eight o'clock and I thought the spell was broken. But Lannie reached over and turned off the radio. He said, "When you were a little girl you used to come in my room and listen to Elvis. Do you remember that?"

"'Heartbreak Hotel,'" I said. He'd had a ukulele hanging on the wall and live turtles in an aquarium.

"How old're you now?"

"Seventeen," I lied. His hand brushed my back.

"Would you do something for me, Kate? Would you take off your glasses."

I took off my glasses, carefully folded them at the temples, and set them beside a stack of cork coasters on the wagon wheel coffee table in front of us.

He stood up, smiling, and took both my hands in his. My knees trembled. With the sponge rollers in my hair, I wanted to hide. I was thankful it was nearly dark in the room.

He said, "Boy oh boy."

"What?"

"You look nice without your glasses."

"Well," I said, "I can't *see* without them."

He laughed and pulled me near and kissed me. This kiss was no peck on the mouth, certainly not a peck. Neither was it voracious or insistent. It was a kiss I yielded into and felt all over my body and I know he felt it, too. For a first kiss, it was just right.

Then there was the rattle of the back door, my aunt coming home. We sprung apart. Lannie nearly leaped to the light switch, turned it on. She came to the door of the sun porch.

"Kate," she said, "I've got news for you. Come sit down in the kitchen with me."

Lannie and I looked at one another, perplexed. I followed my aunt into the kitchen. There was a quart bucket of just-picked strawberries on the table. I sat down. She opened the refrigerator and got out the ice water and poured herself a glass.

"Your mother called Mom tonight."

I had trouble hearing her. In spirit, I was still on the sun porch.

"Are you listening to me, Kate?"

"Yes, ma'am," I said.

"She needs you to come home." My aunt drank her ice water, almost a glassful before she went on. She sat down wearily across from me. She looked very much like my mother at that moment, plumper, more rested, but they had the same frown lines, the same graying cowlicks.

"Is something wrong?" I said.

"She doesn't sound good, Kate. Do you know how to get a hold of your father?"

"No, I don't," I said, ashamed that that was the case.

She sat there mulling over something, but didn't say a word. In a distracted manner, she pulled a grocery coupon from her blouse pocket, tucked the coupon under the sugar bowl.

"Lordy, Lordy," she said. And then finally, "Be that as it may. I've changed your reservation. She wants you to come home in the morning."

She woke me up at five in the morning. I'd had a restless night. I was afraid of what I'd find at home and I felt cheated of the feelings – the sensations, really – that had begun on the sun porch. In retrospect, I think it was probably for the best that my aunt had come home when she had. Though I wondered always about Lannie's intentions, I knew more about my own, and we might have found ourselves in deep trouble if she'd come home a half hour later. While I was eating breakfast, with my aunt sipping her Irish breakfast tea, Lannie slouched to the kitchen door in his terrycloth bathrobe, sleepy-eyed, and with a salute and a wink, he said, "Bon voyage, cousin Kate."

AT HOME, my mother had taken to her bed.

I'd been met at Friendship by a neighbor, a twaddling, bossy woman who offered no word of what I should expect and I didn't want to ask. The first words out of her mouth were, "Well, guess your gallivantin's over with." Her face was rodent-like, shrewd and sly. She had a crucifix glued to her dashboard, and her car smelled cowy. She made butter and cheese at home and delivered it door to door to customers in the surrounding hills. On the hour-long drive from the airport, she told me about some people on her route who'd lost a lot of money playing bingo, money they could ill afford to lose, she said. There were others she ran down. A male elementary teacher who'd moved away for some mysterious reason having to do with a senior girl; a woman whose trash was filled with empty sloe gin pints; another who kept her good furniture protected in plastic. I wondered how much she knew about my family, what she might say to our neighbors. I minded my manners, though, and thanked her profusely. She let me out at the end of the driveway, warning only, "Don't slam the door." I felt irritated at my mother for sending her to fetch me. My heart beat wildly as I approached the house, out of anger I told myself, but more likely it was apprehension.

It was full summer, with the mustard high along the edges of the cornfields, nubbins of green apples clustered on the fruit trees. Joe was up in the treehouse, an encyclopedia open on his lap. He was becoming a bookworm just like me. Maureen and

Colleen had mapped out rooms in colored chalk on the front porch, their playhouse, and Maureen was spanking a baby doll while Colleen stared into a hand mirror, painting her lips in a greasy curve with an old poppy red lipstick. She had on a straw beach hat. They still wore their summer nighties, flowered, ruffled affairs.

When the girls saw me, they dropped what they were doing and ran up to me, for hugs. This made me happy to be home.

"Where're the big boys?" I said to them.

"Riding their bikes," Maureen said.

"David's all gone," Colleen said. Her corn-colored hair had been brushed, but Maureen's had not.

Then I remembered David was away at Student Council Leadership Camp. I realized how trying the week must have been for my mother with David and me away.

"How's Momma?" I said. We were sitting on the stone steps, my arms around them. Bingo lay in a sweaty, panting heap nearby.

Maureen frowned, shook her head. "She's sleeping."

I left my suitcase there on the porch and went in the house. It was cool and quiet inside. In the dining room, no one had cleared after lunch – peanut butter and jam jars were open, bread crusts and raisins littered the table. Dead irises, like tiny gray rags, dried in a milk bottle of cloudy water. Someone had been looking at a photo album, the kind with the snapshots stuck in little black corners. There was a picture of my mother coming out of the water at a lake, smiling in a careless way, a way I'd never seen her.

"I'm home," I called.

"I'm here," she called back, her voice croupy and frail. "In the bedroom."

She was propped in bed against pillows, wearing a frayed

dress shirt of my father's. Her eyes were bloodshot. The curtains were drawn. A week's worth of newspapers lay at the foot of the bed. Six empty waxed milk shake containers were lined up on the blond headboard of the bed, and a Gideon Bible lay open beside her.

She patted the bed. "Come sit here, Kate," she crooned.

I sat down. "How're you feeling?" I said.

"Not so good," she said. "Was grandpa okay?"

I hesitated to answer her. There was a stale smell in the room, like soiled laundry left too long in the hamper. "Everything *went* okay," I said.

She frowned at the door. "Close that, would you?"

I closed the door, and then she said, "Your father was after me all night."

"Is he here?" I said.

"He was in the basement all night," she whispered. "He's after me."

"Momma – he's not here, is he?" I hadn't called her Momma in a long time. I believe at that moment I wanted to be the child again, but I sensed I was being jimmied out of childhood and that she needed me to be the grown-up.

"I don't *know*, Kate." She started weeping then. "Sometimes I can't *tell*."

"You're just tired," I answered. I wanted to believe this. "Tired and worn out."

She took hold of my hand, placed her palm against mine, as if to measure me. Our hands were the same size. Pensively she said, "Truer words were never spoken."

"That's it," I said. "You need to rest." I squeezed her hand. "And not worry."

She lay back on the pillows and stared at the ceiling.

"I'm going to make it nice in here for you," I said. "You

don't mind, do you? If I straighten up a bit?"

She rolled her head side to side, touched my knee. "I don't mind."

"How about some music?" I said.

"No. No music," she said, a trace panic-stricken. "I remember too much."

I was filled with a largess of energy. I thought by the weight of that, my energy, I could make it all better. I'd flown in an airplane and I'd been kissed. There was a generosity I felt, and a certainty, that if I worked hard enough and loved her enough, she would change. I did not know the places in her mind she could go where I would never go. Or where I hoped I'd never go. And when that happened, there was no retrieving her. Coming back was something she had to do for herself. But I didn't know that then. I knew very little of madness, and I didn't want to know about it. I thought I could salvage what was happening. I cleaned her room, and then the dining room and kitchen. I fed my brothers and sisters, ordered them to bathe and shine their shoes for Mass the next morning. I put Maureen's hair up with bobby pins and setting lotion. Kevin wanted to iron his own shirt and I showed him how. I locked the doors at dusk. And I brought my mother pot after pot of tea, held her hand, listened to her ramblings.

The next morning, I brought her breakfast in on a metal Coca-Cola tray she usually kept hung on the kitchen wall. "It's a beautiful day," I said.

She said, "Kate. I've something important to tell you. Sit down."

Her voice was conspiritorial, low. I slipped the tray onto her lap, and I sat down on a bright blue kitchen chair she used for a nightstand. The sun lay in a warm lozenge on the afghan at the foot of her bed, and Rummy slept there in the sun. I thought she must've pulled Rummy up there, for the company.

"What is it, Mom?"

"I've been thinking," she said. She folded and smoothed, over and over, the edge of the topsheet. She'd begun to have liver spots on her hands. "I've been thinking someone needs to be sacrificed."

"What?"

She set the tray on my father's side of the bed. "Sacrifices are called for. In the Bible." She was wistful, slow-spoken.

"Those're just stories."

"Kate, I know what I'm talking about."

"What *are* you talking about?"

"David."

"What about him?"

"He'll be sacrificed."

And this is when I knew that it would be a mistake for me to care for her alone. In families like ours, boundaries blur, and some of the time you cannot distinguish between truth and lying, sanity and madness, right and wrong. You can go on having a life together, pretending. But this was the point at which I was sure she'd gone beyond a boundary. It took this long to be sure.

She frightened me. I'd heard of stories like this before, on the late news, or in crime magazines on the newsstand, a home suddenly turned violent. Something still protected us, though. She'd chosen David and David wasn't there. I couldn't believe she would hurt one of us.

"Here's an egg in an egg cup," I said. "Just the way you like it." I'd given her a red-and-white cloth napkin and rye toast.

"I'm not crazy, Kate," she said. "And I'm not a child."

"No one said that," I said.

"I know what you're thinking."

I did not believe her. I was thinking that I never wanted to be where she was. I said, "What'm I thinking?"

"That mothers shouldn't be like this."

"The kids're getting ready for Mass," I answered. "The priest's stopping by for them. At the main road."

"You better walk them out," she said, driftily, turning to her breakfast.

Before that day was over, my mother had signed herself into a psychiatric hospital. Kevin was an altar boy and I'd given him a note to give to the priest. After Mass, he came to the house. He knew many things about us, as is often the case with troubled families. People who make it their business – priests and teachers and social workers – know the details of your trouble though you've never breathed a word of it yourself.

He spoke with her in the bedroom. I stayed away in the kitchen, scrubbing a cast iron skillet with salt.

He took me out in the yard and said, "She needs help she can't get at home." He was an old priest, with yellowed white hair, sloped shoulders, and a kind manner. He wore gold-rimmed glasses he'd repaired with electrical tape.

"What should I do?" I said, unimaginably relieved that I had someone to ask.

"I think she'll do what's best. I think she knows that," he answered. "I'll drive her myself to the hospital."

Within ten minutes she had packed a small suitcase and said good-bye to those of us who were around the house. She went peacefully, in low spirits. Instead of shoes she wore scuffed pea-green corduroy house slippers. Kissing my cheek good-bye, she said, "Do what makes you happy, Kate. I left out so many things." Her words seemed final, as though she were going away to die rather than to recuperate.

Arrangements were made. A social worker came calling.

The powers that be decided we children could stay together in our home if an adult relative came to stay with us. Spinsterish, afflicted with a near martyr's sense of family obligation, my father's great aunt rode the Greyhound from Evansville to be with us, though she was very old, and hard of hearing, and she shook from Parkinson's disease. She was the only one who would join us, and I was set against her from the beginning because I'd once heard my mother say that this particular aunt blamed her for my father's comedowns. We did not know her well and she did not know us. Moreover, she did not know how to contact my father. She believed in prayer and that is what she spent her time doing. She owned three rosaries, blue glass, wood, and pearl, and she made herself feel more at home by fixing up a shrine to the Virgin on top of the television. A votive candle burned there, above the evening news, above "American Bandstand." She held to all sorts of superstitions and old wives' tales, about evil eyes and blood in eggs. Good things she credited to God's will; bad things were our fault. Rock and roll offended her deeply, handiwork of the devil, she said. I had no patience with any of this. We argued. I said that when I had children – if I ever did – I'd tell them only the truth. They would know nothing of the Easter Bunny or Santa Claus or God or the Tooth Fairy. She persisted in believing I was a good Catholic girl, though I hadn't been to Mass in six months. On and on it went. When I think of the ways I baited her, I am ashamed. Truth be known, I didn't want her there. I made the lunches and suppers, delegated chores. I was in charge and felt invincible and had no faith whatsoever in grown-ups or authorities. As often happens, my empathy comes much too late; how feckless, how green, how burdensome, all this progeny must have seemed to her.

Summer rolled by, my senior year began. We got on surprisingly well; the weekly visits with the social workers went smoothly. Maureen learned to read, Joe won spelling bees, Kevin kept on serving as an altar boy. Stephen and David took a paper route, and on the night they collected, they'd buy loads of penny candy to share around at home. We pretended we were all right without our mother; any mention of her would bring tears to our eyes, especially late in the evening; we avoided talking about her.

At school, I won awards, performed in plays, wrote articles for the school paper. I had a boyfriend who liked me. We never pretended to be in love; we were pals. Our mutual interests were theater arts, World War II, and what I thought of as making out, though we never put words to what we were doing in his mother's car in the depths of an apple orchard after dark. Before going out to the orchard, more often than not, he'd give me a tour of his father's study, the war memorabilia stashed there, Nazi helmets, insignia patches, Japanese buttons and knives. I knew my mother wouldn't approve of what I did with him, the whisker-burned cheeks I returned home with, the chapped lips, but I felt free of that, as though her sanctions weren't important anymore and I were no longer her child. Other times I'd dwell on the blank hole of her absence, and long for what I'd rarely had, someone to rely on, counsel, consistency. If I didn't think about my mother, didn't allow myself to get in a stew about her, the pieces of my existence fit together like a children's puzzle, so long as I had stamina for it all, and when you are that age, energy seems abundant. I was nagged close to the bone only by the thought of college – how would I be able to afford it?

On Sundays, we were taken to visit our mother, and though she would come out to the shady grounds of the hospital, among the birches and conifers, and we would show her our schoolwork and the little ones would tell her of their triumphs and concerns – I myself was secretive, watchdog of my exploits – it always felt as though we were talking through a glass wall. Her medication buffered her from us. Sometimes David and Kevin and I would rove away and peek with curiosity at the other patients, placated, bovine women, sharing sticks of gum and cigarettes, waiting for visitors. Her life there was a mystery to me; she never spoke of it. We were witness to change in her, though – she'd begun to wear her hair differently, in what we called a "pixie," and she'd had a manicure. Eventually, as winter came on, she talked of coming home.

ON PEARL HARBOR DAY we had our first real snow. It accumulated in elegant peaks in the porch corners, covered all manner of junk piles around the houses, making new and bundled shapes that pleased me. Mother had come home that day, and she was there when I arrived from play rehearsal. It was nearly dark outside. David grunted over a snow shovel, paving a path from the front door to the driveway. Inside, there was a fire in the fireplace, a clove smell from the kitchen. Colleen and Maureen sat cross-legged in front of the television, eating warm molasses cookies. My father's great aunt had left the night before, on the bus heading west. She'd given me a book for Catholic girls, about love. She'd said I should think about starting a hope chest.

I ranged into the kitchen, without taking off my car coat. Mother was browning a pot roast in a black Dutch oven.

"Things're moving a little slow here," she said. "I'm not used to being in the kitchen." She seemed optimistic, a touch awkward. She had an apron on.

"I thought we'd have pork chops tonight," I said. "Didn't you see them thawing?"

"That's a fine greeting," she said.

We looked at one another as though we could hardly recognize ourselves. The kitchen was steamy, the hair on her forehead in damp fringy curls. Overlapping cookies, row after row, cooled on waxed paper laid out on the butcher block.

"They might spoil," I said, self-righteously.

"What're you all in a huff about?" she said. "Why don't you take off your coat and stay awhile? You could peel the spuds."

I did as she told me; I didn't want us to get off on the wrong foot, as she might've said. But I felt none of what I'd expected to feel when she returned home. The welcome; the affection; the relief; the praise. *The praise.* More than anything, I'd expected her to tell me what a fine job I'd done, how selfless I'd been. I'd done what I'd done for myself, so my life would go on uninterrupted, but I hankered after her approval, felt cheated of it. She treated me like any other child.

"You'll do dishes, David," my mother said, after supper.

"David doesn't do dishes anymore," I chimed in. "He only does laundry."

"Since when?" my mother said.

"There's a chart on the fridge," I said.

"I don't give a tinker's damn about your charts," my mother said, in a mock lighthearted voice. She lit a cigarette, nervously tapped her lighter on the table.

"It works," I said, incredulous.

"I'm home now, Kate." She blew her smoke toward the ceiling.

I hated her—no, it was more complicated than that, I felt stripped of any glory or authority or value—and I pushed my plate, a little too insistently, until it collided with the lazy Susan in the middle of the table. David got up and began slapping silverware against the plates, mixing the scraps for the dogs into a bowl. We exchanged smart-alecky shrugs.

"Don't get on your high horses," she said.

I lived at home as a near stranger after that, working at the camp on the weekends, staying late after school, keeping up my guard to everyone but my little sisters. I found constant fault with my mother, her way of doing things, but I held my tongue. She served the same monotonous vegetables over and over, creamed corn and green beans with bread crumbs. She allowed sweets before supper. Her drinking picked up again. She encouraged Joe to fight back when he was bullied on the playground. To my way of thinking, she could do nothing right. How unfeeling I was, how arrogant and smug; how much I stored up to regret, enough to last for years.

We had one night of truce, in April. I came home laughing, dancing, jumping up and down.

"I won," I shrieked into the dining room. "I won a scholarship."

She took the letter from me; it was on heavy watermarked bond paper, an important-feeling letter. My brothers and sisters gathered around and she read the letter aloud to them.

"A full scholarship," she said. "That's the finest thing, Kate." She cupped my cheek in her palm. "That's really fine."

I felt shy, embarrassed by her touch, it'd been so long. I turned away, knelt down, and said to Maureen, "I'm going away to college."

"I don't want you to," she said, pouting.

"I'll miss you," I said. "Oh God, I can't believe it."

"I believe drinks are in order," my mother said. She went to the buffet and opened a bottle of sherry. She poured it into two shot glasses; we didn't have the proper ones. The television was on in the front room, big-band music on a cartoon show. My brothers and sisters bashfully clustered around us, diffidently leaning with their elbows on the table. The long window was open and birds were trilling, nesting for the night.

The world seemed luxuriant with possibility. My mother toasted my future, we sipped the sherry, and after a few minutes my brothers and sisters wandered away, and I petted Rummy as we drank, to avoid my mother's eyes. We sat there talking cautiously. She smoked and I fingered a cigarette without lighting it. We had second sherries, this time in the jelly glasses.

"You'll do it all, Kate," she said, "You're my bright and shining light."

I cried then, but I don't believe she saw me crying. The dining room was dredged in a slate blue dusk. In her Baltimore Colts sweatshirt, her cigarette at a jaunty angle, my mother looked to me like a grainy photograph of some other time in my life, a time I thought I was breaking free of, a time I would try in vain to forget.

MY FATHER came home for a visit, the night before prom night. No one mentioned our mother's hospitalization or the months we'd lived there with his great aunt. Perhaps my mother and father had kept in touch all along. I know nothing of that. I only remember the welcome we gave him, festive and cheerful.

After supper, only the three of us were left at the table, my parents and me, drinking coffee with evaporated milk from thick china mugs.

"Kate's won a scholarship," my mother said.

"Good for you, kiddo," my father said. He looked much older than I remembered, his hair nearly white, in a crew cut. He wore baggy green work slacks and a V-neck sweater over a T-shirt. His sight was failing and he'd had to get glasses.

"She's going to need some help, though," she said.

"How much help?"

"I'm not sure," my mother said. "She'll need clothes. And books." Almost as an afterthought, she added, "I don't know how I'll get along without her."

"I've a job there already," I said. "In the library." It gave me great pleasure to lie awake at night, imagining myself stamping due dates inside the covers of books.

"She'll still need money," my mother insisted.

"We'll have to see about that," my father said.

His tone, the inconclusiveness of his words, stirred up uneasiness in me. I excused myself and went out to the porch. No one was about. The grass was deep in the yard, and hadn't been cut yet for the first time that year. I took a yellow canvas camp chair out into the grass and sat down not far from a stand of irises. To calm myself I thought of the prom, the library job, my graduation dress, swatches of dream I handled over and over in my mind, for comfort.

Ten minutes later my father came up behind me, touched my hair, his hand gentle, tentative. Even now, after all this time, if a man touches my hair I am moved to tears, and I will, more often than not, find myself falling in love with that man.

"Your mother still needs you, Kate," he said.

"I-won-a-scholarship," I whispered deliberately.

He took his hand away. "You don't know how strapped we are."

I stood up, faced him, my arms folded across my chest. The men in my family are short and stocky, and I had grown – I was nearly as tall as he was.

"I can't help that."

"Your mother still needs some help." He said this in a voice intended to be appealing, his hand on my arm, pressuring.

I yanked away. "You can't stop me."

"Why not put it off a year? She wants you to think about

that." A pickup truck went by, switched on its tallowy head-lights. His eyes were trained on the road, not on me.

"She *doesn't*."

"She asked me to ask you."

I raised my arms and clenched my fists. "I'm going," I pitched at him, screaming. "*You* went to Labrador."

He looked surprised, bilked in some way. Then he slapped my face hard, hard enough to make my sight go reddish black for a brief moment. He'd never done that before.

The shock of it fired through my body, and not just the slap, but what I'd done to provoke it. *Honor thy father and thy mother* popped into my mind. I planted myself there, stoic and con-fused and crying, my shoulders hunched and hands stuffed in my pockets. My nose ran, but pride kept me from wiping it.

He pinched my chin and said, "Look at me, damn it."

I silently refused to open my eyes.

He booted away the camp chair, then hustled quickly into the house, swearing under his breath, the keys on his belt loop clinking. He slammed the front door.

It was a warm spring night and if I try to imagine it, I think the Japanese maple leaves were probably just beginning to un-furl, like little brick-colored boats, and my brothers might have been playing catch. But I saw none of that. My senses were shut down and I felt only that slap and its ineluctable wake, a convic-tion that I *must* leave. I told myself he had no claim on me. When you are seventeen you have no idea what people and places will claim you, own you, forever. And though I didn't go away to college until after Labor Day, my connection with my parents was severed at that moment, not to be healed for many years. My father went on the road again two mornings later, and I lived at home that summer, working nights at a soda fountain, sleeping late, reading in bed, hard feelings, sad ones, lodged in every corner of the house, every place I turned.

Since then, I have always wanted to be the one to leave. Sometimes I think there must be tricks to leaving, to keep the hurt at bay. But my father never told me if there were, and I have spent a lifetime trying to find out.

Love You Can't Imagine

IN SMALL TOWNS you never know who will appear from out of your past. You give up being vigilant about it, you just expect to have to confront mistakes you made, dead-end roads you drove down way too long. Sandra thinks this – *there's a living, breathing, dead-end road right before your very eyes* – when she sees Tom Crib in the light of a pink Japanese lantern, on the veranda of the cabin where the cast party is getting underway. He's in a rocking chair, drinking Moosehead beer, snuggling a little boy in his arms. The boy looks to be about two years old, with Tom's whitish-blond hair, but curly, cherubic.

"You were fantastic, Mom!" Desiree squeals.

Sandra had the female lead in *Take Me Along*, the community theater's major summer production, and this was the end of the run, a Saturday night in late July, Chelan, Washington. She arrives, contented, modestly proud, exhausted but wired, trailed by a devoted mélange of supporters. Kelly Ford, a trail crew supervisor, whom Sandra thinks and speaks of, a little self-mockingly but lovingly, as her beau; her seventeen-year-old daughter, Desiree, and three of Desiree's friends, all of whom are dressed in tony vintage clothes, shorty lamb jackets, petite hats with black veils, print silk dresses, big pearl and rhinestone clip-on earrings, kid gloves; her sister Pat and her ten-year-old son, Roger, who sat through the entire performance listening to Bob Marley and the Wailers on his Walkman; and Easy Whip, Kelly's rotund lumbering malamute, with his sleet-colored eyes. He didn't name the dog; his ex-wife did. They are tramping up the gravel drive toward the friendly lights of the cabin, the aluminum beer keg in a tub of ice, the members of the cast and families and friends already gathered there, the slapping of the lake water against the shore, where it's promised, later, they'll have a bonfire. They had to park the van near the county road and the drive is lined with cars and pickups. In wind blowing off the lake, the rotting lodgepole pines creak like old bones.

"Thank you, sweetheart," Sandra says to Desiree, reaching for her, curling her hand around Desiree's. Their fingers feel chilled in the mountain night air.

Pat swats her affectionately on the fanny. "The theater in you's finally coming out," she says. "You were terrific."

Once Sandra had thought about becoming a clown. She imagined starting her own small business – Clowning Around she'd have called it – to entertain children at birthday parties. She knew she had theater in her. She'd been in one-act plays in high school, The Lottery and The Open Window, but those were cloying with heaviness, with meaning. Clowning Around would've been light and breezy and the laughter of children would have followed her like hummingbirds after honeysuckle. Now she has a job she likes, GS 6, Secretary, Forest Service District Office.

She hides her face behind the quilted lapel of her ski jacket. "I don't know if I can take any more attention," she says.

Kelly says, "Buck up. You deserve it. You were terrific." He draws Desiree and Sandra in close for a hug, says, "Listen, girls,

I spied T.G. out back. I'll be there helping him with the fire. If you need me." Easy Whip trots behind him, around the frost-tinged poppies, the flowering butterfly bush. On uneven terrain in the dark, Kelly has the walk of an arthritic dancer. He's paying for all the times he carried murderous sixty-five-pound packs into the backcountry. A worn hip joint causes him increasing pain as he grows older – he's forty-two – yet still he walks with grace.

Desiree squeezes her hand and offers Sandra a secret womanly smile, meant to convey how much she understands that Kelly loves Sandra. Desiree is pro-Kelly all the way. She brainstorms wedding plans. Not a week goes by without her saying, "He's truly a nice guy, Mom. Look at the way he treats you." Usually Sandra will answer, "You don't have to convince me."

At the veranda they go their separate ways, Roger to the wide steps where he sits down and picks through the stock of cassette tapes he's brought along, Pat to the knot of people around the keg at the far end of the veranda near the hammock (her husband's on a canoe trip in the Yukon and she misses him, but she's determined to have a good time without him), the girls inside to the stereo where they will jockey for control of the music. Sandra feels momentarily abandoned.

"Here she is – queen of the hop," Jerry – the play's director – says, saluting her with a red plastic cup of beer. It's his cabin. She thinks of Jerry as an older man; he took early retirement from teaching high-school speech and drama in Seattle.

She kisses his cheek. "You brought it out in me."

Then she meets Tom's eyes.

He says, "You hid your light under a bushel for a long time."

She feels defeated and put down by his first remark. How does he know she hasn't starred in every play of the past decade? "I'm surprised to see you, Tom," she says.

He rubs the sleeping boy's head. "We're just passing through. On our way home from Spokane."

Inside the girls have put on Tracy Chapman. They seem to be moving into a social awareness stage – watching the news on PBS, saving money to go to a Farm-Aid concert – and Sandra's pleased by that. At the keg someone is singing, slightly off-key, not quite sober.

> Oh the women
> > are all fat in the ankle
> > and they all
> > kind of droop in the can.

Jerry says, "How do you two know each other?" He takes off his glasses, eases one side of his shirttail out of his khakis, and wipes the lenses with the shirttail.

"You first," Sandra says, skittish, suddenly tongue-tied. "How do you two know one another?"

"Tom's wife, Debbie, was a student of mine," Jerry explains. "It's funny how these things happen. I was in the Nickel Ad office a few days ago, trying to compose an ad for a boat I'm selling – that Fiberglas canoe – the blue one – and lo and behold, in they come. Debbie, Tom, and Lance here. You know Rick. At the Nickel Ad. He's Tom's brother."

"Small world, as they say," Tom says. "This's my boy, Lance."

"He looks like a real sugarpie," Sandra says.

"Are those girls your girls?"

"Just one," Sandra laughs, and she sounds phony to herself, thinking, Don't you remember anything? "Just Desiree. When it comes to plants and pets and kids, one of each seems about right to me."

And she casts about for ways to extricate herself – a friend, or even an acquaintance, will do. She keeps thinking, What's wrong with this picture? People change, just like Pat always insists. It's possible, they do. The miracle of human adaptation never ceases to amaze her. There was no mistaking his love for the boy and she feels glad of that. For the boy; for his wife; for Tom himself. Though she feels cheated too, infected with a selfish streak of wondering why he couldn't have been that way with her. With Desiree. When they needed it.

She squats down and says to Roger, pressing her finger to his chest, "Aren't you freezing with just that T-shirt on?" She can smell the watermelon gum he's chewing.

He can't hear her; under a reggae spell, he has his headphones on. "Batman," he says.

Kelly peeks between the dowels of the veranda rails. "Sandra. Sugar. Why don't you come on around here and help us out?"

She figures they are smoking a joint. "I'm on my way," she says, relieved.

"Whoa," Jerry says. "Not so fast, young lady. Come again. How do you two know each other?"

"From the old days," Tom says.

That about covers it, Sandra thinks, the bad old days. She steps off the veranda onto the path, zips up her jacket. "We met there too, didn't we? At the Nickel Ad office." She's aiming for a devil-may-care tone, but she's not sure it comes across.

"Sure enough," Tom says. And just before she turns the corner, he catches her eye. "Let's talk. Okay? In a while?"

"Let's talk, Tom. Fine."

Her high heels sink into the pine duff on the path. She wonders what they will say, what they can possibly say after all these years. Pat would say, A lot of muddy water passes under the bridge in twelve years.

Around the corner Kelly and T.G. are between the cold

frame and the compost pile, huddled over a joint, trying to light it. Kelly circles her in a bear hug from behind, lifts her off the ground, snacks on the nape of her neck. He says, "Here's my partner in crime."

She twists in his arms, kisses him on the mouth. His nose is cool, his skin smells like the woods.

"You guys are great," T.G. says, then, parenthetically, passing her the joint, "Special occasion." Getting stoned has become a once-in-a-while treat for T.G. and Kelly, and usually she turns down their offer to join them. Sandra has even given up her nightly Watneys Red Barrel in favor of a clear head every morning. But not tonight; tonight she'll have a ritual toke. T.G. is a drummer in a country band, president of the local Sierra Club, kindergarten teacher, and Kelly's younger brother. He's after them to find him a woman. He says he wants what they have. "How do you do it? How do you *maintain?*"

"True love," Kelly says. "True love, my man."

And Sandra feels that same physical stirring, quickening delicate as a fern's shadow, a gleam throughout her pelvis she always feels whenever Kelly speaks of his feelings for her. He is a man who knows the aphrodisiac women can't resist: freewheeling conversation about feelings, dreams, desires. One of Kelly's dreams stands in the way of them moving further into their lives together. Kelly wants a baby and Sandra is sterile. "You knew that from the get-go," she always says to him whenever he talks about his confusion, his inability to relinquish the option of being a father. "Indeed I did," Kelly will answer. "I shook every apple off your tree anyway." It's true; he'd shaken her to her roots.

Sandra's love for Kelly is not the sort you hear about in songs on the jukebox. It's not desperate or crazy. They met three years ago and it was one year before they made love. Kelly said he wanted to get to know her first and Sandra thought that was a novel idea. When she remembers that year going by, she imagines ranging in the high country on a long hike, when it's tough-going at first and you don't know what to expect. Maybe you slip and fall when the trail crosses a creek bed, maybe the first lake is small, disappointing, but you push yourself, you glory in the little things along the way, the shooting stars and glacier lilies, the marmot whistling, and before long, just as you are simply traveling, putting one boot in front of the other for the bliss of it, you come upon grand peaks and a string of alpine lakes so rare and peaceful that you imagine no one else has ever been there before you. It's where you belong. That's what being with Kelly is like. Easy, once you reach cruising altitude. Paradise, kind of. And ordinary. Common pleasures renew them. Razzing one another; watching a video in their bathrobes; dividing the foxglove in the fall; lying awake in one another's arms at midnight, waiting for Desiree to come in from some breakneck double date. Love you can't imagine when you're young, when you think that love is you winning him over, a treadmill of pursuit and chicanery.

SANDRA'S LINEN SKIRT was soft, worn, a Jonathan Logan she'd bought at a church rummage sale for seventy-five cents. She ironed it on the kitchen table, sprinkling it with water from the tap, then steaming out the wrinkles. The pleasant hot earthy smell of the linen – like grasses in sunlight – rose around her as she ironed. The people in the next apartment were listening to "60 Minutes." She'd taken two Advil for the menstrual cramps that'd begun right after the car broke down.

Tom Crib would be back any minute and they were going to see *Annie Hall* at the dollar theater on Main Street. This was their first night in the studio they'd rented; new town; new apartment with a pepper tree in the courtyard; new landscape. No one knew where they were or how to get a hold of them, and they liked the freedom of that. They'd driven from Bishop all night on two white crosses a hitchhiker'd given them. Tom said they shouldn't take them, you can't trust hitchhikers. Sandra said she trusted this one, he was A-OK, she liked the way he shared his six-pack and he didn't throw the empties out the window. They'd eaten the white crosses and the talk had picked up, accelerating through their memories. The Volvo was jam-packed with their belongings and had out-of-date '77 Colorado tags. Sandra and Tom had been picking apples in Washington, near Brewster, and when that ran out they decided to "check out California," drive the length of it to see if they might like to settle there, in some small town in the Sierra foothills or the Owens Valley. Tom knew bookbinding, and a little about photo-offset. He wasn't afraid of heights and knew how to trim trees. He was confident he could find work, enough to get by on. Sandra talked about starting a business. Maybe she'd be a clown for children's birthday parties.

"You need wealthy people for that," Tom had said. From a café in Lone Pine he called a buddy of his in Palm Springs – someone from the old days in Seattle – who said he was thinking about starting a small press to publish guidebooks. He said, Come on down, the weather's fine.

When the car lost compression and died, about four in the morning, they'd pushed it onto the sandy shoulder near Yucca Valley and hitchhiked into Desert Hot Springs, figuring it would be a cheaper place to live than Palm Springs. It was a Sunday, and there was not much they could do about the car on a Sunday. They took the first apartment they looked at, unloaded the few things they'd brought from the car in rucksacks, and settled in, more or less. The studio was one small room, with a kitchenette and brown shag carpeting and brown nylon furniture. In the cupboard there were Teflon pots and a skillet – the Teflon crosshatched with scratches – an iron, three plastic coffee mugs, and an open box of roach poison. The table where they ate was next to the double bed. Someone had left a Baptist Church calendar from two years back nailed to the wall. There was no phone, but the landlord had pointed out a pay phone just across the road, near a coffee shop whose windows were boarded up with warped plywood. It hadn't taken long to hang their clothes in the closet, stack their books on the orange plastic Parsons table.

Sandra was reading a book about starting your own business, Tom was reading *Black Elk Speaks*. They'd met some people in the Okanogan Valley who lived year-round in a tipi and sometimes they talked about doing that. It seemed a hard road to turn down, surprisingly complicated and pricey and fraught with tough luck. You were always at the mercy of the weather, and living in a tipi was one strike against you from the beginning with most people, people who thought you were just plain lazy to want to do such a thing. Still, it was a dream they toyed with, a way of whiling away otherwise dead time.

She wondered if her ex-husband, Ranny, would let their daughter visit her if she lived in a tipi. Desiree was five years old. She lived with Ranny in Chelan, where he was foreman at a big peach and cherry orchard. With a steady job, legally he had the upper hand. All that stability – the job and a new wife with two children of her own – couldn't be argued with. Almost everyone – Sandra's mother, Ranny, Sandra and Tom – conspired to believe that this was the reason Sandra did not have her daughter. Only her sister, Pat, guessed that there was more to it than that, but Sandra wouldn't talk about it. She felt blackhearted, paralyzed with self-inflicted hurt, when the other reasons danced mockingly before her in the dark late at night. When that happened, she'd get up and drink hot milk and rye to bring on sleep.

As she ironed, she fiddled with the dial on the radio. All the stations carried a grisly story of two women who'd been killed during the making of a snuff film on some beach near L.A.

Tom walked in with two brown bags of groceries.

"I'm not sure southern California's my idea of California," she said. She thought of northern California, the soft shapes of ocean fog, the land's nooks and crannies. She thought she might prefer that to this blond desert, these infertile hills.

Tom squeezed by to set the groceries on the counter. "I bought a barbecued chicken," he said.

"It's hollow-feeling out here, Tom. It's like an empty gym." She held the skirt up by the waist and eyed it critically for wrinkles.

With a paring knife, Tom slit open the cellophane package of chicken. "It's what you make it," he said.

She thought it could be an argument about to happen and she didn't want that. She was dependent on him now and it's much easier to have arguments when you have friends and family nearby to salve your hurt, to take your side. Here she knew no one. They'd had some bad fights. And usually she would pick up and leave for a while, hitch a ride from Brewster down to Chelan and visit Pat, or take Desiree on the boat ride up the lake, just to calm down.

"You're right," she said. "I'm just adjusting."

They ate the chicken and Sandra worked at ignoring the cramps.

Tom said, "I tried to call Bill. His phone's been disconnected."

"He was your only lead here?"

"Pretty much. I'll just start making the rounds tomorrow. After I get the car back."

"How'll we get the car?"

"I guess we'll have to pay a wrecker to bring it down here."

Sandra thought of the four-hundred-thirty-two dollars remaining in their kitty and the strange landscape—the Joshua trees like mannequins among the scurfy blocks of quartz monzonite. Reading the free brochures from the tourist office, knowing the names of plants and rocks and radio stations and streets—all that helped. It was the amorphous unknown that left you floating face-down in anxiety. She wondered if she'd made a mistake, if she'd known Tom long enough to move more than a thousand miles away from home. They'd been together sixteen months. He was thirty-six and still a wanderer. She'd had a job selling classifieds when he'd sashayed into the office to visit his brother, who owned the Nickel Ad tabloid she worked for. Maybe moving in itself was a mistake, no matter who you do it with. She catalogued the moves she'd already made in her life—always they were moves from someone or something, never to something. She'd moved away from home to escape her mother's carping; to shed a rough reputation, she'd moved away from Ellensburg, where she'd studied accounting for a year; and she'd moved away from Chelan because that was too close to Desiree. Tom withdrew whenever Desiree was around, and when Tom withdrew she went crazy with wanting him with her again, and that became the thing she needed and craved most, Tom's presence, his touch, his hard body, the sex, him coming into her, distant as he was. Men were like that, she told herself—most men were, anyway. She could still depend on him. He hadn't said she had to choose between him and Desiree, but he didn't want any family responsibilities. He'd been frank about that, he always reminded her. She thought he might change. She had the idea that they were going to settle down together. It's easy to quit your job in the summer, when the days are long and hot and there are river parties and potlucks and you can hitchhike easily anywhere. But now it was almost winter, their second winter together, and this hand-to-mouth life was no life for a little girl she told herself. She looked forward to going to the movie, she wanted that escape from the confusing ricochet of her thoughts.

Against her skin, the linen skirt, the rose silk blouse, felt good. When they left the apartment Tom took her arm in a courtly gesture. The cool desert wind flung sand against their legs. Halfway to the theater, a squat fiftyish woman in sunglasses, lugging two bright yellow shopping bags, stopped and sharply wrenched her face up at them – like a bird – as they passed her on the narrow sidewalk. "Healthy, healthy, healthy," the woman clucked.

They sat on the aisle near the front. Tom draped his arm over her shoulder and secretly, softly, brushed her nipple. That irritated her. Her cramps were reaching into her now, like a hand grasping. And lately, whenever he touched her there, she remembered her recurring nightmare: her breasts sliced away, gone, gone.

The lobster got away from Woody Allen. A biting pain fixed Sandra – pinned her in wonder – and she could no longer call it a cramp. "I'll be back," she said.

In the restroom she leaned on the sink, quivering, pressing the heels of her hands against the cold porcelain. A Planned Parenthood decal peeled away from the mirror. Her face in the mirror was bloodless, greenish in the fluorescent light. She'd never faced anything this wrong before. It was taking her over and felt like the end of something.

She walked down the aisle to Tom, each step deliberate,

measured. She eased into her seat. "I'm sick," she said.

"What?"

"Let's get out of here," she said. "Please."

She leaned on him as they made their way to the back of the shadowy, nearly vacant theater. The light from the movie glazed the faces of the people in the back rows. The popcorn in the lobby smelled almost rancid.

Outside, the sidewalk seemed to draw her down to its gritty surface. Tom held her up. "This is bad," he said.

"I need a hospital," she said. "I want to lie down. Right here."

"Jesus. We don't have the car." He scouted up and down the street. "There's a cop. Betcha he'll help us."

Sandra crumpled to the curb and leaned against the cool steel of a parking meter. Peacock blue streaked the sky, the wispy clouds like tail feathers. There was no traffic. The harsh lights from the marquee cast deep shadows of the palm trees beyond the theater. As though he were under fire, Tom ran in a crouch to the black police car.

The pain cracked through her now. She doubled over and wanted to lie down. Some sense of decorum kept her from it. She hadn't let go of all that yet and maybe that meant it wasn't so bad, whatever was happening.

Tom walked back in long strides, his arms open to her all the way across the street. "Let's go," he said. "He's taking us home. An ambulance'll meet us there."

The police car seemed to move in slow motion the five blocks to their apartment, the radio spitting broken messages.

"If anything bad goes wrong," she whispered, "would you do something for me?"

"What's that?" he whispered.

"Tell Desiree I do love her. Even if she doubts it."

"Don't think the worst."

"You will, won't you?"

"It's okay," Tom said. He had his arm around her.

At the apartment they waited three or four more minutes until the ambulance arrived in a wave of white and red noise and light. The ambulance attendants took over her body. The dry palmetto leaves rubbed in the wind like insects burring, and the wind slipped into the ambulance with her. They slammed the door.

Tom was in the front seat. She could see the back of his head, his pale hair. She was flat on her back and rocked in the swerves of the ambulance turning. One attendant knelt beside her and took her blood pressure, and then said, "This is Demerol." He wiped her inner arm with alcohol.

She culled a joke from the whole deal. "Hit me." The dark-skinned attendant smiled beneath his sparse moustache. Streetlights rushed by, like hot apples. She couldn't pick them. She could never pick enough apples to make a living, to make do. He covered her with a wool blanket and the Demerol leached through her.

In the emergency room they rolled her onto a high hard examination table. Tom had disappeared, though she could hear his voice nearby, just around the corner it seemed, answering questions. She knew they'd be asking him about money, about paying for things. She curled into a fetal position. That seemed to diffuse the pain just a little. The pain crackled like lit gasoline in line with an explosive core just above her pubic bone. She was cold. The walls were cold blue and they made her cold.

"She's shivering," someone said. It seemed to be the same woman who whipped the green curtain around the rods above the table. "Roll over on your back, honey." The nurse nudged her over and covered her first with a stiff sheet and then a wool blanket. She lifted one of Sandra's arms from under the blanket and laid it in a straight line along her side, the inside of the elbow up and exposed. "Leave that there," the nurse said. "Someone'll come along soon with an IV."

Every time the nurse came near, Sandra smelled the faintest film of soap on the nurse's skin, like a spice. The bluish tubes of light above her hurt her eyes. She was afraid of closing her eyes, afraid of going under. People seemed to be milling about beyond the curtain and she heard the low murmur of decisions being made. She could hear the voices but not the words. An infant cried out in a keen squeal. A new nurse – a man with gray-blond hair and rough blotches on his cheeks – rolled the IV beside the table. The Demerol was doing its work well. Sandra didn't feel the punch of the needle in her vein. The soft place on her inner arm where the needle went in, like the underbelly of a kitten, looked puffy and torn. It was a big needle.

She drifted, not awake and not asleep. She had the idea that Tom had left her there, that he'd gone to fetch the car. They needed the car. She felt a hand on her forehead and opened her eyes. Tom towered over her, still in his 60-40 parka. His belt buckle was a brass elk head. His gaze flickered up and down the length of her and she tried to make eye contact with him. He looked frightened.

"What's wrong with me?" she said.

He put his hands in his pockets. "They don't know yet. The doctor's coming."

"I want my mother to be here."

"We're out of control here, aren't we?"

"It'll be all right, I think," she said. Later she would remember that, the way she wanted to help him out, to make it easier for him to deal with the hospital. She could've died from the infection, but when she saw his addled innocence, his fear, the way his eyes were glazed and empty, as though he might just neatly break away from what he couldn't control, she rose up with reassurance. That scared her more than anything–the idea of Tom breaking away.

THE MOON is a few nights past new, a sliver, shining on the black and moiling lake in an iridescent waver. They have the fire going now, a big one, a Billy Blazer Kelly calls it, and he launches into tales of his Boy Scout days, the jokes they played on one another, the blistering ill-equipped hikes. He and T.G. can entertain one another for hours like this and Sandra enjoys it–she's warmed by their rough and tender affection. The party's noisy behind them, fifty yards away. T.G. sits on a log across the fire from Sandra and Kelly, poking at the coals with a rusty branding iron, rearranging a chunk of wood here, a twig there.

"So I'm changing the subject," T.G. says. "Mom and Dad were here when you were building trail last time. They rented an RV. A mo-ho Mom called it. They were headed out to the Olympic Peninsula for three weeks. Dad's stomach is giving him fits."

"Stress?" Sandra says.

"He sounded stressed out on the phone last time," Kelly says.

He slips his arm around Sandra, kisses her cheek, a habit of his. Then he reaches into T.G.'s cooler for a beer. "Sandra?"

"No thanks," she says. She imagines T.G. and Kelly's father–his seriousness, his bluff, his surface talk.

T.G. gets up and rummages in the woodpile for a particular size log, returns to the fire and seeks out just the right place for it. Orange blossoms of sparks fly.

"What do you guys think about this? Give me your honest

opinion now. It'd be easy to scoff at this, I know – more hippie-skippie New Age rationalization – but in my men's group someone said that when we get sick you can think of it like a metaphor. For something else in your life."

"A metaphor?" Kelly says.

"Yeah. A metaphor." T.G. is warming to the subject now. He's wearing melon pink climbing pants with a drawstring waist and he hitches them up determinedly and reports, "It's like this. It's simple. Dad's stomach is bothering him, right? That means – it's possible now, it's not out of the realm of possibility – that it means there's something in his life he *can't stomach*."

Kelly pats his own thickening waist. "Like if you eat too much it means you're hungry for something else? Your spirit's hungry?"

"*Exactamente*," T.G. says.

Sandra thinks that later she'll ask him what it is he's hungry for. She pulls out her mittens and puts them on. She hears footsteps and turns to see who's coming.

"What do you think Dad can't stomach, T.G.?"

"I'm working on that one," T.G. says.

Tom and his wife, Debbie, step into the firelight. Tom keeps one hand at her elbow, and under his other arm he's carrying a lumpy cotton sleeping bag. She's pregnant and her due date must be near. She's wearing a flowered shift and knee highs and a black denim jacket. Her shift pulls up high in the front, inches higher than the back hem. Tom and Sandra do the introductions all the way around. No need – right now – for Kelly to know who Tom is in relation to her. She's given him a crash course in all that transpired in her life before she met him, but she's never mentioned Tom by name. He'd become ancient history by the time she met Kelly. Tom shakes hands with T.G.

and Kelly, then he unrolls the sleeping bag on the sand and helps Debbie settle down. She's young and still has a sprinkling of acne on her sunny round face.

"So where's the little one?" Sandra says.

"He crashed out," Debbie says. "Dead to the world." She has the distracted look of women about to deliver, as though she inhabits a supercharged inner world of such change and subtlety and potential intoxication that the mundane holds little allure.

T.G. has turned away, looking for wood ostensibly, but Sandra knows him well enough to know he feels their private family talk has been interrupted and he doesn't like it. She can sense Kelly's eyes on Debbie—no, not on her, on her pregnancy. Then he fools with the fire, intuition at work; he doesn't want to hurt Sandra with his musing. She can see all this in the silence that ensues. She's been connected to these boys too long not to understand.

At last Tom asks Kelly a question and they begin talking about trails. It's trails versus roads. And they move on from that to conservation in general, and from that to hunting season and Fish and Game regulations, a predictable conversation. Sandra thinks there's a certain security in listening to their talk; and she's allowed to simply drift, to measure metaphors against memories.

THE NURSE yanked open the curtain and the doctor entered. He was a big Indian man, with straight black hair and a smooth hairless face. He reminded her of someone she'd seen at a powwow at the Sheraton in Spokane.

"When we finish here, prep that baby for the meningitis tests," he said to the nurse. He picked up Sandra's chart and squared back his shoulders, rolled them, as though trying to shuck off tiredness or tension, Sandra imagined. He'd spilled something brown, coppery, on his white jacket.

"You'll have to leave," the nurse said to Tom, and Tom disappeared. She closed the curtain and said, "Pull your knees up and scoot your bottom to the edge of the table."

Sandra did as she was told, though moving was slow, clumsy. She tucked her heels in the stirrups at the corners of the table. The blanket piled up on her stomach and the cool air made goose bumps on her inner thighs. The doctor touched her thigh with something chilled and metallic.

"That's the speculum," he said.

Her muscles involuntarily tightened, clenched, at the foreign touch.

"Let go," he said. "Try breathing deeply. Relax."

The speculum was inside her now. Under his breath, almost inaudibly, the doctor said, "Christ on a crutch."

The nurse stood beside the doctor, staring over Sandra's knees into her eyes, chewing the inside of her lip. Her flamered lipstick was almost worn away and she had the lines of a long-time smoker around her mouth. Sandra thought, She knows what it's like.

"We've got to get that IUD out of there." He rose from his stool far enough to lock eyes with Sandra and say, "You've got a dangerous infection. I'm going to pull that IUD right now."

"All right," Sandra said. And she did feel something, just a tug, something sharp, and liquid running from her, blood she imagined. She tried to picture the IUD: a dark red rag. Then there was the sound of some small thing—like a trinket or a charm from a charm bracelet—being dropped into a metal container.

The doctor was by her side. "I'm going to start you on antibiotics," he said. "We'll do some tests in the lab to make sure—

but it looks like PID. Pelvic inflammatory disease."

Then he too was gone. The nurse covered her up again and slipped through the curtain. Sandra wished Tom would come back and be there with her. She wanted comfort, she wanted someone to take care of her.

At four in the morning they went home in a taxi. The doctor had given her instructions to take the antibiotics, the pain killers, to drink liquids, to rest.

"I thought they'd keep you there," Tom said, supporting her as she undressed and sank into the bed.

"We didn't have any insurance," she said.

For Sandra, the next three days passed without structure, without domestic rhythm, with no definite demarcation between sleep and wakefulness. She stayed in bed, did not have the strength to get out of bed, and she wandered, drugged, on the outskirts of consciousness, of making sense. The meds blurred her vision and she could not read. She could not make it to the bathroom on her own. She depended on Tom to carry her there, to support her there while she tried to urinate. She knew it was night when Tom came home from looking for a job. She knew it was morning when he left. Before he left he always said, "You sure you'll be all right by yourself?" And she always said, "Sure. Go. I'll be all right." Though she did not really have a sense that she would be all right. She knew she was still in the part of the sickness where she could go either way. She drank quarts of fruit juice over ice and none of it was coming out of her. When she tried to urinate, there was only a trickle. Her abdomen swelled and she was frightened. She had waking dreams, hallucinations: standing with Tom under an arbor of bones, a black train bearing down on the Volvo; searching for Desiree in a place where children had been found in an abandoned icebox.

The third afternoon he hauled in all their belongings from the car. He brought in his .22 and stood it in the corner. It was a Remington his grandfather had given him and the receiver had been specially engraved somewhere along the line with curlicues and his grandfather's name. Sandra was awake enough to pay a kind of oozy attention when Tom carried in all her things she liked and had forgotten she'd brought with her: the tape player and the Kate Wolf tapes, the wooden Asian tea box she kept her correspondence in, her calligraphy pens, her velvet cape, her hiking boots.

She watched him make a tuna sandwich and sit at the Formica table, eating and reading the want ads. The news was on the radio. Her sheets were damp with sweat and she wanted clean sheets, but she didn't want to ask for anything. Her skin felt hot and abraded by fever.

Once Tom went over to the door and opened it and just stood there, staring out. "I'm glad we're on the edge of town," he said. "We can see the sun set."

"Is it a good one?" Sandra said. Her abdomen was rounded, tight as a drumhead, and she stroked it, wincing, as they talked.

"It's a very good one." Tom pressed his hands high against the door frame and leaned there, one knee cocked. His leather printer's apron lay beside him on the floor. "Dates grow all around here," he said. "I'd like to get some." There was the sound of singing from a nearby apartment: "What a Friend We Have in Jesus." "The landlord's a Bible thumper," Tom said, closing the door.

"Help me, Tom," Sandra said.

He carried her to the toilet and she felt her life depended on whether she could go.

"The poison's trapped inside me."

Tom had his hand on her shoulder.

"I'm afraid it'll kill me. If I can't go."

He stood beside her and waited. She hated for him to see her the way she was, sour and infected and weak. She knew she shouldn't think of that right now, there would be time for that. She focused all her attention on ridding herself of the infection and at last, she was able to urinate, for a long, long time.

"Thank God," she said.

"Do you think you can sit at the table?" Tom said. "I'll change your sheets."

She sat at the table and drank a cup of tea and then he helped her into the fragrant bed. She felt lighter, stronger, more clear-headed. She realized how much of getting well depended on taking responsibility for it herself. No one could do it for her. She thought about the word *responsibility*. Responsible. Responsive. Respond. Respond to yourself. Tom went in the bathroom and she could hear him shaving, the squirt of the shaving cream, the scrape of the razor. The singing next door had ended, and the wind blew the swaying pepper tree.

Tom came out of the bathroom and sat on the edge of the bed. He lit a cigarette. He had on clean jeans and a pale blue plaid Pendleton shirt. His face was a handsome one she never tired of. His hooked nose had been broken twice in wrestling injuries in high school. His lips were full – good kissers, she always thought.

"I'm going out for a while," he said.

"Where to?"

"Just out. I need to get out."

"I'm better."

"I can see that," he said. "I wouldn't leave you if I didn't think you were better."

"Put on a tape for me before you go," she said.

Sandra knew she'd passed over into healing. Her fever was

down and she worry warted about Tom. That was a luxury she couldn't have afforded a day earlier. Tom was a track in her mind she could get on and travel without ever getting anywhere. She was lonely without him. Even sick, she could work herself into arousal thinking of the raw shiver of her skin when they'd had sex for hours, remembering making certain sounds, pretending until pretending made it so, until she would do anything he asked, try anything, say anything. To him, she called it making love, wanting him to hear the word *love* from her, wanting to think it would actually make him love her. Between them they had private words for it. To herself, she was more blunt, she called it having sex. She missed doing it; that was the only time she felt close to him. There was something shameful about that, she thought. She'd never admitted that before; it's possible the meds had cut her defenses, let light into her interior monologue. And then, after an hour or so, she surprised herself by thinking that she might be lonely if he were there. Maybe it was something in herself she was lonely for, some way she had an inkling she was capable of being, but that she couldn't be with him. She wished she could talk to Pat, who was always good company, even if she was probing and plainspoken, too tactless sometimes. They'd always been able to commiserate together, against parents whose wrangling took all the emotional energy they could muster, against adolescent boredom, against harsh weather.

Tom had left the tape player near the bed and she could change the tapes herself. She thought of better times when she heard the music, and almost any time in her life could be considered a better time than this. Careless wild road trips she'd taken; the way the light hits the forest at dusk in the Cascades—green-black and mysterious; and Desiree, how much trust there was in her yet, how serious her voice sounded as she learned her numbers. With a little prompting, she could count to one hundred. The thought of her daughter, the sweet and perfect line of her jaw, her breath like sour warm flowers when she'd crawl in bed with Sandra in the morning–that thought bloomed into a physical longing and fear, fear that she'd never have that again. She was a mother who'd left, and that made her an outlaw of sorts. And outlaws have to run hardest from themselves.

Tom came in around eleven, his key quiet in the door. She'd left the bedside lamp on and she'd been drifting after taking a Tylox at ten o'clock. He hung his parka in the closet, went to the refrigerator and opened a beer. Sandra sat up against the pillow. Rain pelted the flat roof. He came over and sat on the edge of the bed again and patted his pockets until he found his cigarettes. He held the pack to his mouth and drew out the cigarette with his lips.

"You're back."

He lit the cigarette. "How're you doing?"

"Okay."

"You're going to wear out those Kate Wolf tapes."

"They're a consolation to me."

"I went to a bar." He took a long slug of the beer. Then he drummed two fingers on the side of the can.

"Was there music?"

"Yeah. Some band from L.A. The Whitewalls, or something like that."

"Did you dance?" Sandra said. And she knew as soon as the words were out of her mouth that that was a question she didn't really want to know the answer to. She ran a finger along the double side seam on his jeans.

"As a matter of fact, I did."

He cut the ground out from under her with that. For a minute, she felt as though someone were pressing hard on her chest. She felt invisible and weak. It was stupid – overreacting – to feel jealous or envious – whatever it was – over such a small event. She pitched down the feeling. When she was stronger, she'd pick it up again, try to take an honest look.

Tom said, "I just went out and did what I wanted to do."

She had to assume that if he'd done what he wanted then, that he was home now, doing what he wanted.

"At least we're not pretending," she said.

"That's right."

Last year, after Pat'd been divorced and changed jobs twice in three months, she had been in counseling. Sunbathing in her backyard, eating corn chips and cottage cheese, with Desiree splashing in a plastic pool, they would often pick over these counseling sessions, on the lookout for choice morsels of wisdom. And her sister had said that pretending was one way of being in the world that could cause you plenty trouble in the long run. That made sense to Sandra at the time, but she'd forgotten it until now. You could pretend for only so long, and then you split open with the truth. That kind of truth – the kind you've sat on for months, maybe years – hurt everyone too much. She thought of moving back to Chelan. It was possible there were chances in the world you could take that might bring good luck, moves that could bring you closer to yourself.

"Are you sleepy?" Tom said.

"Not really."

"Maybe I'll read to you. Would you like that?"

"Yes, I would."

Tom sat in the overstuffed chair next to the bed and sipped his beer and read to her from *Black Elk Speaks*. He had a good reading voice and she could picture all the things he read about. At the end of the chapter his voice cracked and she looked up to see that he had tears in his eyes.

"It's not the life I bargained for," he said.

Sandra murmured, "That makes two of us."

She'd never seen him cry. He closed the book and sat there, sadder than she'd ever seen him.

"Why don't you come to bed?" she said. "You've had a long day." They had news to break to one another, but all that would keep until tomorrow.

The next morning, before dawn, Tom got up and went out with his .22. While he was out, Sandra was able to go to the bathroom, able to brew a pot of coffee. She looked in the mirror at her lank and greasy hair and resolved to take a shower first thing. She opened the venetian blinds and peeked through the slats. She thought she might be able to make it to the pay phone later in the day. The date trees were gray-blue and huge against the lustrous pink sunrise. Presently Tom came into view, his gun at a angle to the ground, a rabbit for their supper dangling in one hand.

She could call collect. It would be better to call collect than not to call at all. She could start with her sister, who'd be cheerful, theatrical, who'd say, You ninny, where on God's green earth are you?

IT'S LATE. Debbie has laid her head on Tom's lap, a signal, Sandra reads, that she's ready to leave. Sandra thinks she and Tom probably will not talk, and she is neither glad nor sorry. She tries to imagine what they might say, what phrases they might grab for to sum up that time, to excuse it, to tuck it away in memory where it wouldn't cause too much havoc in the day to day. Clichés of that era come to mind, for it does

seem another era: we were too young (not true); we didn't
know what we really wanted as individuals; words they might
have already said that next morning to begin the breakup. She
doesn't want to say these things; they seem off-center from the
truth, not quite congruent with what she feels. What she feels is
that everything that happened back then – leaving Desiree, am-
putating herself from the past – was no one's fault but her own,
and that she has nothing of value to say to him, nothing. That
doesn't seem right somehow – as though they should have
things to say – but it's true. It's herself she has to answer to every
livelong day; that's enough.

More people are around the fire now, talking hushedly,
some of them holding hands, some of them drinking beer.
Near the quaking aspen, two dogs tussle over a weathered coyote skull. Kelly and T.G. are out at the lake's edge, with T.G.'s
arm over Kelly's shoulder. Kelly's pointing out a constellation
to him. His shiny down vest glistens in the moonlight.

Sandra remembers what the doctor said when she returned
to Washington State. "You have to have a hysterectomy. We'll
do it vaginally. There'll be no scars. No visible scars." That was
in the spring; there was still snow in dirty patches on the doctor's lawn. She sat down there anyway and cried, waiting for Pat
to drive up and take her home.

And later still, years later, she brought suit against the company that made the IUD, and it's still pending, tied up in the
courts with thousands of others. Kelly made her do it, not for
the money – there wasn't a chance of being awarded big
money – but for the principle involved. She'd told him, "I'm
not sure I want more babies anyway." And he'd said, "That
should be up to you to decide. Up to us."

She wants to be the first to leave the party, and she doesn't want to make the rounds saying good-bye.

At the lake's edge she says to Kelly, "Could we go soon? I'm about to turn into a pumpkin."

"It's past this scout's bedtime too," T.G. says. She kisses his forehead.

"Getcher crew together, babycakes," Kelly says. "I'll meet you out front."

On the veranda Sandra's slipped out of her heels—they'd been killing her—and she and Desiree are sprawled on the glider, waiting for the others. Roger's gone—crankily—to collect his mother and Desiree's friends. His cassettes are scattered all over the steps. Paper plates of leftovers—celery stubs and cracker crumbs—are piled on a wooden end table. Desiree's makeup is smeared, her daubed-on fake mole streaks like a comet tail across her cheek.

"I've been here so long, Mom—all my life," Desiree says, "do you think I'll ever leave?"

"You might. It's hard to tell. What wayward wind might blow you somewhere else."

"I think I'd always come back. It's my security blanket."

"That's one way of looking at it. A good way."

Kelly comes upon them, whistling for Easy Whip, limping a little, his face broad and serene and ruddy. He jumps up on the veranda, boots thumping.

"Just think about this, Sandra," he says. "Don't say anything yet. Just put this in your pot and stir it. What about a Mexican baby. Or Romanian?"

"What about it?" she says.

"We-could-get-one," he explains, smiling. Then he shouts, roars happily, "We've got goddamned government jobs."

Sandra laughs. "You'll have to talk me into it," she says. She closes her eyes, sighs deeply, and with her bare sore toes pushes off, nudging the glider a little harder.

Desiree abruptly hunches forward, brakes the glider's swing, her eyes glinting with excitement. "No, no, wait," she says, alert and eager, one hand on Sandra's thigh, the other waving Kelly in, the way you direct someone maneuvering to park in a difficult spot. "I'll work on her, Kelly," she promises. "I'll really really work on her. You'll see."

Kelly says, "Good girl."

Sandra feels the shock of blood ties, like standing with them, hands linked, under a waterfall. Bracing, joyous rush, O heady love.

Cargo

SOFT SPIKES of hollyhocks grew along the side of the raft company boathouse. I sat on a flat stone just up the rocky slope, thinking about my mother dying and reading a biography of Katherine Anne Porter. The book would absorb my attention for a few paragraphs; then my thoughts would wander away. Whenever I thought of Mother I remembered a time when I was eleven and the wood delivery truck could not make the slick and treacherous hill to our house. My brother Christopher and I hauled that wood in red-wagon loads and wheelbarrow loads. I remember that we were cheerful about the work at the beginning, but as evening came on and the driveway iced over, we could not be cheerful or glean whatever virtuous feeling we got from being helpful. When I thought of Mother, I felt eleven years old again, and that saddled, that played out.

I'd spent the evening before in helpless long distance conversation with my mother and my sister in Wenatchee. My mother had said, "I'm just waiting to die." I'd heard this from her before, but this time the facts were laid out like quilt pieces, cut already, beyond redesign: the heart attack, the two weeks in intensive care, the emphysema, her fingers stained yellow with nicotine. My sister said she had started smoking again as soon as the hospital attendant removed the oxygen tent. The will to die was strong in her, inevitable as winter, and none of us had ever been able to coax her from death's promise. Suzanne was on her way from the Olympic Peninsula, Jan Mary was already there, Christopher would fly in from Portland on Labor Day, and Laura Jean still lived at home.

"Will you come?" Jan Mary had said, without hope or despair.

I felt nitpicky, asking, but I said, "Is this it?"

"Not necessarily," she said. "We just want everyone together one last time."

"Where's Dad?"

"He had to go to Spokane. With a friend. He'll be back tomorrow night."

She sounded protective, making it sound as though he had business there. I right away assumed he'd gone to play the ponies.

"I have to see," I said. "I'll be in touch." It was the best I could do.

Mo was my friend, a boatman, and he squatted on the boathouse porch, patching a Havasu. A few of the white letters had peeled away from the raft: BIG SKY WHITEW-R. Near the porch steps, peeling red oars were laid in a row across two sawhorses. The radio rippled soul music from Jackson Hole. Wiley sanded the oars. Wiley'd been around since before my time and Mo's time; he'd been the one to show us the ropes that first winter Mo and I were snow-coach drivers in the Park. He'd been the one to lead us on our first illicit after-dark visit to the hot pots. Mo and Wiley had been my buddies, but I was no longer in their daily lives. I'd become the break in their routine whenever I passed through. Clouds like garlic bulbs swelled over

Electric Peak; rabbitbrush was brightly staggered on the hills. I had a view of the arch at the Yellowstone Park entrance and a lone antelope grazing there, her markings ancient and striking and incongruous against the buy-me clutter of Gardiner, Montana. I waited to have dinner with Mo.

The deputy, whose office was at the opposite end of the boathouse building, stepped outside and righted a trash barrel that two dogs had rummaged in. I imagined the blind eye the deputy must have had to turn to cohabit with raft company personnel. Mo's baggy purple shorts caught my attention as he jumped down from the porch and discreetly visited the latrine area, a strip of grass between the building and a blue-and-white school bus.

Mo and I had met as young and eager poets in grad school in Missoula. Halfway through the first year, he dropped out and moved to Gardiner and he had lived there ever since, river-guiding, working the winter season for the park, never writing another poem, though he would read my poems and give me a tough response.

He picked his way up the slope, evading cactus.

"Que pasa, Roxie?" His hair was the palest red, shiny as embroidery floss, and he was beginning to bald. His arms were powdered with fine sawdust, and his hands smelled like the solvent he'd used to clean the abrasion on the boat.

"Just waiting for you, Morrison."

"Louisa's invited us for dinner." Louisa was Mo's mother-in-law from his marriage to Sharon, who had died in a car accident in the Gallatin Canyon. Sharon and Mo's daughter, Celestial – Cee-Cee – lived with Louisa.

"I can't stay long," I said.

"You'll stay the night, won't you? I want to play with Cee-Cee awhile," Mo said, crouching down until our eyes were level. He rocked my knee with one hand. "How're you doing?"

"I'm okay."

"I know this's not what you had in mind. But I haven't gotten together with Cee-Cee all day. We'll go to my place after."

"It's okay."

"You don't sound like it's okay."

"I'll just be here tonight," I said, shrugging. I couldn't stay in Gardiner more than a night or two. My welcome there was long worn out because of things I'd done that winter, the winter we were snow-coach drivers, things I was ashamed of now. If I stayed too long, word got around and people showed up and reminded me of pieces of myself I wanted to forget.

"Porter, huh?" He picked up the book and skimmed the blurbs on the back. "What's her story?"

"She lied about a lot of things." He handed me the book. I said, "How is Louisa?"

Mo stood up and reared back, flinging his arms as though about to break into song. "Louisa. Louisa's a wonder."

"How so?"

"She's become a Keeper of the Flame."

"What's that?"

He quoted officiously, "Keepers of the Flame is an international organization. They use affirmations and meditation to change what they don't like about the world situation."

"What don't they like?"

"Nuclear weapons. For example."

"What can I say, Mo? You've got a crazy family. Your mother-in-law meditates. Your daughter plays with trucks."

"Safeway let you off?" He was referring to my half-time produce job in Bozeman.

"For ten days."

"Ya-hoo."

"Ya-hoo, you yayhoo." I felt tender toward him at that moment, for the way he feels for other people. He always finds something to celebrate. I said, "I'm hungry. How long do we have to be here?"

"Let me put some tools away. Come on down. Shoot the shit with Wiley. He misses you."

"Where's Sally?" I asked. Sally was Mo's sweetheart, a bareback rider in the Wild West Show in West Yellowstone. She wore turquoise leather hot pants trimmed in white feathers. Before each show she slathered her legs and arms and face with pancake makeup the color of cloves – the show's producer, an ex-carny barker, wanted her to look native. Once when he was a little drunk on whiskey ditches, Mo confided that the color turned him on.

"She's working," he said. "Last show of the season."

I gathered up my things, relieved to know Sally was in West and I'd have Mo to myself, once we negotiated dinner with Celestial and Louisa. I had nothing against Sally. It was just that Mo had been my friend for over ten years, whereas she had been his lover for two. It was a question of shared history – we had it, she didn't.

Mo went on down and shouted to a woman standing in the door of the boathouse. She gave him a thumbs-up signal. Wiley boogalooed in tight choreography to Gladys Knight and the Pips. The deputy came out again, hitched up his brown trousers at the pleats, and got in his pickup. I felt as much an outsider as the antelope, though she could trot away into the backcountry, free of the obligation to be civil and free of the past. I envied her that.

I waited in the passenger seat of Mo's van, with the door hanging open. A scroll of charcoal smoke breezed our way from a nearby house, and the scent hinted at childhood parties, blistered hot dogs, sticky s'mores, the marshmallows crisp and black. Two girls walked by, about twelve years old, one of them skinny and one of them dumpy already. I'd seen her type too often at Safeway: old at twenty-three, pushing a cart filled with babies and beer. They both wore outsized flannel shirts cinched with wide patent leather belts, their new school clothes I imagined. The skinny one said, "He knows I'm alive." Wiley looked up and waved to me. I waved back and thought, That's about how much he misses me.

LOUISA'S HOUSE was a collector's item, with a sculpted gate of rusted scrap iron, the porch pillar carved in a totem pole of cats' faces, a mass of fuchsias in hanging baskets, and a blue enamel Home Comfort stove like a shrine to warmth in the kitchen. What was once the living room had been divided into shelf after wooden shelf of stock for her mail-order business, The Unicorn's Horn. She sold metaphysical books, crystals for healing, tarot cards.

"Make yourself at home," Mo said. "I'm going over to the Conoco for a bottle of wine."

I went in the kitchen, stood at the sink, and watched Louisa and Celestial through the screen window, in the garden on their knees, digging up carrots. The kitchen smelled like brown rice steaming and overripe vegetables. Near the phone there was a framed black-and-white photo of Sharon, pregnant, in a Panama hat, drinking a St. Pauli Girl. Sharon had been the best of Mo's women. She didn't let marriage slow her down. Three years after her death and I still half-expected her to walk in at any moment and charm me into going out dancing.

Four-year-old Celestial had on pink-and-lavender overalls and a Yellowstone Raft Company cap. She sang, "I'm a little tea-pot, short and stout," over and over in a squeaky thin voice while Louisa gave her instructions: "Dig down deep or you'll cut them in half. Shake off the dirt." A small black goat nibbled nearby on red cabbage leaves.

"We planted enough for Choo-Choo, didn't we, Louey?" Celestial said. Choo-Choo was the goat.

When Celestial looked my way, I waved. She stared through me, ignoring me. I felt hurt – she'd known me all her short life. I wondered if she was beginning to see me as an intruder. There was an invisible connection among Celestial and Mo and Louisa, some faith created, simply by living in proximity for so long. I saw what I'd given up by leaving and I'd left so many places, thinking to begin my life again, forgetting every time that the things you hate the most are the things that travel with you.

"I'll tell Daddy about the bear," Celestial said, confidentially to Louisa.

"Wonder if that rice is done?" Louisa said.

"I'll check it," I called, and Louisa acknowledged me with a wave and a nod over her shoulder. Her coarse hair had begun to look more gray than black.

Mo walked in and said, "*Pinot Noir*. This place goes all out for the tourist trade."

ON THE WAY to Mo's from Louisa's, he recited from *All My Pretty Ones*: "The town is silent. The night boils with eleven stars./Oh, starry, starry night! This is how/I want to die."

I felt cynical and said, "There's a storm moving in."

Mo's apartment was over a Laundromat. Until eleven at night you heard the slosh of the washers, the hum of the dryers. We poured more wine and sat in the dark at the kitchen table, the bathroom light angling around our feet. There were three ragged marigolds in a fruit jar on the dresser. Soon after we came in, the rain began and lightning cast flashes on the creamy curtains.

"Tell me about Anne Sexton," he said. "When you heard her read."

These were our favorite stories.

"It was in Baltimore – "

"Once upon a time in Baltimore."

"People were like leeches at that reading. Everyone wanted a piece of her. She was fragile – in a red dress – she'd have called it a sheath."

"Tell me again what she said."

"She said, 'Writers should be forgiven their bad books.'"

"Sad," Mo said, kneading his earlobe.

This seemed an appropriate time to tell him. "I have some bad news, Mo."

"What's that?"

"My mother's dying."

He reached across the table and sheltered my hand with his. "I'm sorry, Roxie. This's been coming, hasn't it?"

His words – or perhaps his touch – primed my tears. My chest felt hot, heavy with burning cargo. I went to the counter, tore off a paper towel, and wiped my eyes.

"I can't decide whether to go. I can't stand to see her the way she is."

"What way?"

"You know – I've told you. All tanked up on Thorazine and bourbon. Shut down."

"She's had a hard life, Rox."

He spoke the truth. I folded my arms and didn't say anything.

"Have you thought about how you'll feel – years from now – if you don't go?"

I sat back down. "Tell me how it was when your mother died."

He sucked in his breath, then sighed. "I've told you before."

"Tell me again."

Mo got up, turned off the bathroom light, and lit a candle. When he took his seat again he said, "She knew she was going. She insisted on being at home. The doctor agreed." He poured himself another glass of wine. "I just went home for the summer. With Cee-Cee."

"What did you do there all summer?"

"I read to her. Listened to her when she meandered. Went hiking with the baby – Cee-Cee was just a baby then. I needed the connection with both of them."

We didn't talk for a few minutes. I scanned the titles on his bookshelf above the table, which was weighted with the West: Snyder, Hugo, Hammill. I picked up *Petroglyphs* and read the poem about the midwife in the tavern. I imagined her at the Town Tavern in Port Townsend, at the wide shiny tress of a wooden bar, fog bleeding under the door.

"She wrestled with dying," he finally said.

"My mother's wanted to die as long as I can remember."

"She might still need you," he said, tentatively, his whisper silky against the wooly thunder.

"She's lost to me, Mo," I said, more surely than I felt it. For years I'd thought of my mother and myself inhabiting a range of labyrinthine mountains, creatures whose paths never crossed. Perhaps we wandered by the same boulder or lake, the same memory, but not at the same time.

"Write about it. Isn't that what you always used to say?"

"I'm not there yet."

"You'll get there," he said.

We were quiet. There was no noise but the thud and muffle

of the washers spinning. Then he said, "Hey—I bought a second hand copy of *The Bell Jar* last week. I bought it for the dust jacket. Remember that picture?"

I shook my head.

"It was taken when she was a guest editor—whatever they call it—at *Mademoiselle*. The photographer said, 'Show me how happy it makes you to write a poem.' And she smiled then. A lovely smile."

"We all smile then."

"Sure-fire smiles."

We could hear a laundry cart being whizzed around the tile floor downstairs, the dryer doors slamming.

"You'll write again, won't you, Mo?"

"It's a spiritual quest, Rox. I'm not on it."

"You've set some limits."

"*Recognized* my limits. I just want to see my daughter grow up in a place where she doesn't have to be afraid. Ski. Bring Sally coffee in bed. Read the *Times* now and then. To keep from becoming a total barbarian."

"I want to go to Ketchum."

"What for?"

"To see Hemingway's grave."

Mo laughed. "It's much easier to go see the dead than the dying." He swallowed a mouthful of wine and pursed his lips. His raspy laughter had broken the tension of the talk about writing.

"Come with me to Ketchum."

"Sally's coming over for Labor Day."

I pouted, half-faking, half-meaning it.

Mo stood up and came over beside me and hugged my head against his belly. His belt buckle pressed my shoulder.

He said, "Let's camp out on the floor. We'll roll out two sleeping bags like puritans and hold hands."

"Twist my arm," I said, looking up at the candle flicker on his face. He smelled like river water and sun and wine. "Do you have any cigarettes?"

"That bad, huh?" He weaned away and browsed in a basket on the counter. "Here's a few Camels." He tossed the crumpled pack on the table in front of me. Someone had slipped a book of matches from Harrah's inside the cellophane. "Some guy left those here. The bullwhip expert from the Wild West Show. He whips them out of Sally's mouth."

I lit the nasty cigarette and smoked it without inhaling.

"That's what's killing your mother, right?"

I nodded and tried to blow smoke rings. "Let's not talk about it anymore."

At one-thirty in the morning, Mo watered his houseplants, shuffling in his stocking feet from clay pot to clay pot with a half-gallon Almaden bottle. I lay down on the floor, on his swirling antique carpet. It made me think of Willa Cather's house. Mo and I had once driven nonstop to Red Cloud, Nebraska, during a drought summer, in temperatures in the hundreds, just to see her house. We were good pilgrims then.

"I have an idea," he said, blowing out the candle. "Let's put on Santana. Very low. And drift away." The care in his voice almost made me cry again.

We laid out the sleeping bags side by side. He put on *Moonflower*. The storm had stopped and the wet cool smell of the rain and sagebrush rolled in the open window. When we lay down he took my hand; hard oar calluses padded his palm and fingers.

I said, "Do you remember the time we tried to make love?"

"You betcha."

"Your tongue felt as impersonal in my mouth as a doctor with a tongue depressor."

"You really know how to hurt a guy."

"We're not meant to be lovers. In the strictest sense of the word."

"Some love's like that. It doesn't engage your lust."

"When's Sally coming?"

"In the morning."

"I want to be out of here before she comes."

"Sally likes you, Rox."

"Her kindness kills me."

"You should let her like you."

"I should be on my way to Ketchum."

When I was a girl there had been an old woman named Mrs. Higginbottom who lived down the road from us. She lived alone in a dirty house with her hunting dogs; she was a bird hunter and would go out, wearing a shapeless housedress and her apron, in the early morning mist along the creek with her shotgun. She hunted grouse. I did not like drinking water or lemonade from her greasy tumblers; I would pretend to sip from them. She had a big black-and-white rooster who charged me if he caught me lolly-gagging in the yard. Nevertheless, I visited her at least once a week. Growing up the way we did, not knowing from one day to the next what to expect at home, we learned to get what we needed – attention or sameness – from our neighbors. Mrs. Higginbottom played her 78 RPM records for me, those heavy ones: "Pistol-packin' Mama." "The Old Lamplighter." She sat smoking Lucky Strikes in an overstuffed chair whose nap had long been slicked down. The smell in her house was an accretion of sweat, old paperbacks, wet dog, and chicken feed. She talked to me about her life as a young woman. She did not seem unhappy to be in her seventies and alone. I understood that there were choices to be made about the way you lived and what you thought about the way you lived. This lesson kept meeting me in a new disguise. It was the central lesson in my life and I the dunce and fool of the heart who could not get it straight.

I imagined the journey, first to Ketchum, then to Wenatchee, the frugal western towns along the way–Rexburg, Boise, LaGrande–wild with autumn leaves. I would give my mother Mo's comfort, a gift like carried fire, protected over the miles. If she wouldn't take it, my brother and sisters could have it. We would be together one last time, not children anymore, no longer yoked to anyone or anything, no longer shackled except to whatever sore memory we hoarded like misers.

"You won't like it there," Mo said. "This isn't nineteen-fifty-nine. There are too many Beamers."

"Beamers?"

"BMWs." His voice sounded dreamy; he was falling asleep.

I squeezed his hand. Like a bad habit I said, "Don't worry. I'll expect the worst."

Same Old Big Magic

H E K E P T the maps. They'd had a cardboard Kahlúa box of maps, forest service maps, topo maps, road maps, some of them from the early sixties when his parents had taken him and his brothers on road trips in the summers. She had to admit they were mostly his maps, though she'd grown to love them, their gift of anticipation, their memory of blind stabs at settling down, of wilderness euphoria. After thirteen years the Kahlúa box was soft as dish towels along the corners.

"T H A T ' S M Y favorite boulder in the Cascades," she told her sister. They were both on the wagon, drinking cranberry tea and talking early marriages. "We camped under it in February one year and walked up into the mountains and hugged trees." Her sister said, "You were stoned, right?" "Yeah," she said, smiling and shaking her head yes and flipping the photo album page. "And we lived to tell the tale."

H I T C H H I K I N G can make you hate one another – or forge a link between you that can't be broken. They had taken two major trips by thumb: one from Oregon to Arizona in the middle of winter and one from Lumby, British Columbia, to Seattle, also in the winter. During these trips, life went on. They made love in the A-frame North Face mountain tent; she complained about how cramped she was on top. She sometimes cried at night, missing her sisters. They fed fragile, hopeful camp fires, drinking brandy and talking, weaving the toughest cloth of their fears and desires, finding out what they believed in. They fought over whether to eat in a restaurant or cook over a camp fire. They never had any money to speak of, but there was a stamina to their love. They prided themselves on having endured. Seventeen below; Nevada; camping in an arroyo among cages of snowy sagebrush. That's love of a different color, her girlfriends said. Hard-core. They did it to see Monument Valley in the winter, rime like crystal sugar everywhere. They did it because they thought they were both born to the road.

ONCE THEY HAD a cabin with a big black Monarch cookstove. This was in the beginning. Lightning pinwheeled into their bedroom and he leaped from the bed and found a book of poems and read her a poem in the storm. They carried water from the creek and shared a zinc tub of steaming bathwater. She scrubbed his back with a loofah. They made love in the parsnip patch in broad daylight. At night there were always the stars and he knew them by name. At a garage sale, they bought a cast-iron skillet and an Oriental rug. From secondhand hardbacks, they read short stories aloud to one another. There were always pileated woodpeckers, red whips of willows, evening sunlight only a gold band above the mountain; there were always animal tracks, lichened stones, creeks, applewood, fir, wild plums; there were always, always, the stars, and his arm around her as he named them: *Orion, Cygnus, Sirius*. He smelled like Balkan Sobranie tobacco and wool Woolrich shirts, and his arms were archetypal arms, arms of the woodsman who'd saved her from the wolf within.

THE DAY they moved away from the cabin they stood on the porch and cried in one another's arms. That was the first loss they'd ever shared, shocked at its sweetness.

IN TOWN, the first town, the elementary school blazed white as sand in the winter sun. He was a student at the college and she taught at the elementary school. Kites tattered from the cottonwoods beside the playground. Their wantonness required practice. "Talk to me," she said. "You have to have a bit of the ham, the rake, in you to do this. Coax me. Be sly. You know how easy I am." Beyond the shutters an evening snowstorm muffled streets; all the cars had forgotten how to travel; they moved as though forced awry by enchantment, into berms and woodpiles. "The words," she said, "can be about how much you know I'll like it." "How does it feel for you to come?" he said. "It's like stealing something." "Stealing home," he said. She was a marauder, slip of a woman in the flying night, stealing whatever she could, fingers tender and blind, grafting bliss to truancy, crazed absence of self. It was something like an old blues song: that bad, winsome, visceral. She knew how it worked. They found them – the very words – and they became his charm and code, his mojo, sweetbone totem, the rib and thorn in their fenny winter bed.

THEY EACH had private dreams and these were difficult to realize together. The first time she talked about moving away, she cried into a brakeman's bandana until her eyes were puffy. Finally he said, "Maybe it's a good idea. Maybe I need to be on my own too." She said no. She said she'd figure out some other way to make her dreams come true. That was in the second year and they had eleven more years to go.

FOR A LONG TIME they took turns moving for one another; the one who followed always felt cheated.

EVEN NOW, when she peruses certain maps, she imagines all the places they slept outdoors together. Beside rivers, with that rushing, that glassy green blooming of the waves: Clark Fork, Gallatin, Yellowstone, Lochsa, Columbia, Methow, Okanogan, Entiat, Wenatchee, Skagit, Rogue, Klamath, Williamson, Santiam, Umpqua, Bella Coola, Fraser, Thompson, Quesnel, Chilcotin. Too numerous to mention were the creeks and lakes. And the mountains they ranged: the Cascades, the Rainbows, the Monashees, the Purcells, the Selkirks, the Tobacco Roots, the Big Belts. Field mice; blackened pots; wood-smoked sleeping bags zipping together; their breath visible in the mornings; aspens shimmering; cutthroat winds. They were caught in the bite of the mother's moon tooth.

AT SHI-SHI BEACH near Neah Bay, they slept together outdoors for the last time. To the Indians, shi-shi meant "big magic." The unrestrained Pacific dumped rain on them four days running. Deer cavorted in the surf. They visited a man in a nearby cabin and drank mescal and traded life stories and waited out the weather. He was drunk enough to eat the worm. She has a crescent-shaped scar—petite petroglyph—on the back of her right hand, from falling into a rocky rain-swollen creek on the walk out. She thinks it's a scar that won't fade and that pleases her, to have the mark of shi-shi.

BEFORE THAT particular July, for several years, they practiced moving away from each other. They were getting used to the idea. First there were separate pleasure trips. Then they began going away to work, a month here, two months there, a summer. Finally she took a job in another state, seventeen hundred miles away. They thought they could manage; they were good at reunions.

THEY BROKE the rules like pottery, with that little regret. Their letters of breakup crossed in the mail, one of many blessings that befell them over the years. When next they met – after the divorce was final – they were rife with happy grief, a blessing in itself they realized. He lived in a small wooden house beside a gang of McIntosh trees. The apples were nearly ripe. The whole tiny house smelled of fresh pocket bread; he baked bread so often that the muslin curtains gave off the odor of yeast and sugar. They cried, made love, slept. They had left an open bottle of Polish vodka on the kitchen table. Once, in the middle of the night, she went out to the screened-in porch. An inverted yellow kayak glowed under the clothesline. She couldn't deny feeling free, a kind of joy in the soles of her feet. The night had grown frost on the dull grass; smudge pots tilted under the trees. Stars stirred above them like fading fires, trying to focus through mottled clouds. This is how she thought of the stars: blurry, a little drunk, still there.

About the Author

Patricia Henley's first collection of stories, *Friday Night at Silver Star* (Graywolf, 1986), won the Montana First Book Award, was selected by the American Library Association as one of the thirty Most Notable Books of 1986, and was featured as an "Editor's Choice" in the *New York Times* and *Publishers' Weekly*. Her work has been published in the *Atlantic*, the *Boston Globe Sunday Magazine*, *Northwest Review*, and other magazines.

She grew up the oldest of eight children in a Catholic working-class family, attending the public and Catholic schools in Indiana and Maryland. She received her M.A. from The Johns Hopkins University. Her obsessions, other than writing, include hiking and travel. Her son, Charles Michael, is a student of philosophy at the University of Montana. Patricia Henley teaches in the Creative Writing Program at Purdue University, and she divides her time between Indiana and the American West.

This book was designed by Tree Swenson.

It is set in Joanna type by Typeworks

and manufactured by Edwards Brothers, Inc.

on acid-free paper.

Other Books in the Graywolf Short Fiction Series